By Alasdair Gray
Novels:
LANARK
1982 JANINE
SOMETHING LEATHER
POOR THINGS
A HISTORY MAKER
Novellas:
THE FALL OF KELVIN WALKER
McGROTTY AND LUDMILLA
Short story books:
UNLIKELY STORIES, MOSTLY
LEAN TALES
(with Agnes Owens and James Kelman)
TEN TALES TALL & TRUE
Verse:
OLD NEGATIVES
Polemic:
WHY SCOTS SHOULD
RULE SCOTLAND

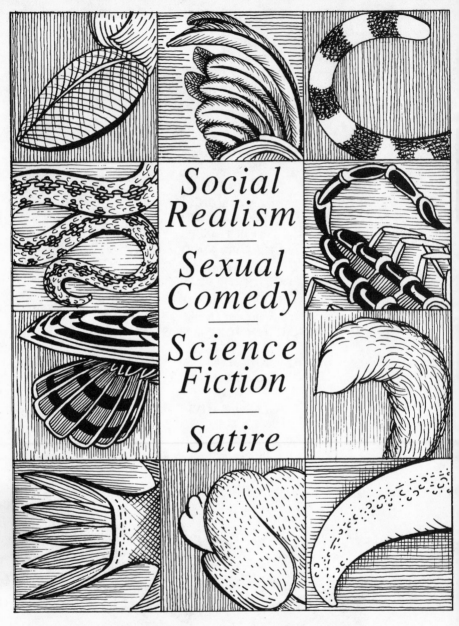

Social
Realism

—

Sexual
Comedy

—

Science
Fiction

—

Satire

A Harvest Book
Harcourt Brace & Company
San Diego   New York   London

TEN
Tales
Tall
&
True

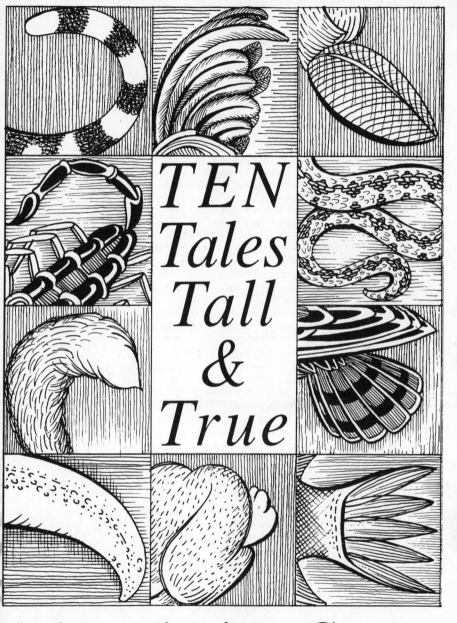

TEN
Tales
Tall
&
True

Alasdair Gray

Eight of these tales have already been published: A New
World in *Fiction Magazine*, March 1987; The Marriage
Feast, entitled Jesus Christ, in *The Sunday Independent*,
17 March 1991; Homeward Bound, *New Writing*, Spring
1992; Loss of the Golden Silence, *Bête Noire*, Christmas
1992; Houses and Small Labour Parties, *Living Issues*,
August 1993; You, *Casablanca*, May 1993; Mr Meikle
and The Trendelenburg Position, *The Glasgow Herald*,
Summer 1993.

Library of Congress Cataloging-in-Publication Data
Gray, Alasdair.
Ten tales tall and true/Alasdair Gray.—1st U.S. ed.
p.   cm.
ISBN 0-15-100090-5
ISBN 0-15-600196-9 (pbk.)
I. Title.
PR6057.R3264T46   1993
823′.914—dc20   93-40980

Printed in the United States of America
First Harvest edition 1995
A B C D E

TO • THE
• ONELIE •
BEGETTERS
OF • THESE
• STORIES •
TOM
MASCHLER
• AND •
XANDRA
HARDIE
• AND •
MORAG
McALPINE

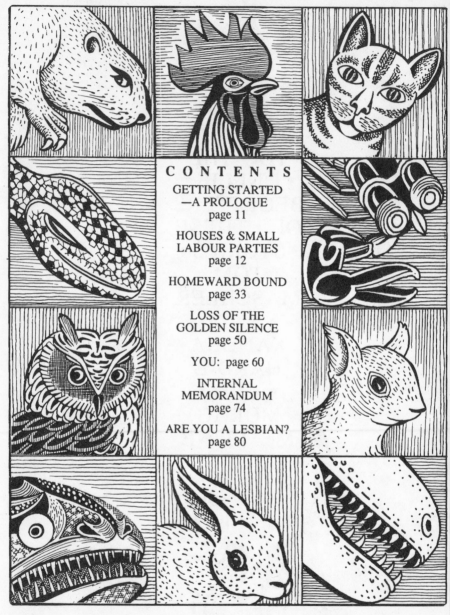

CONTENTS

This book contains more tales than ten
so the title is a tall tale too.

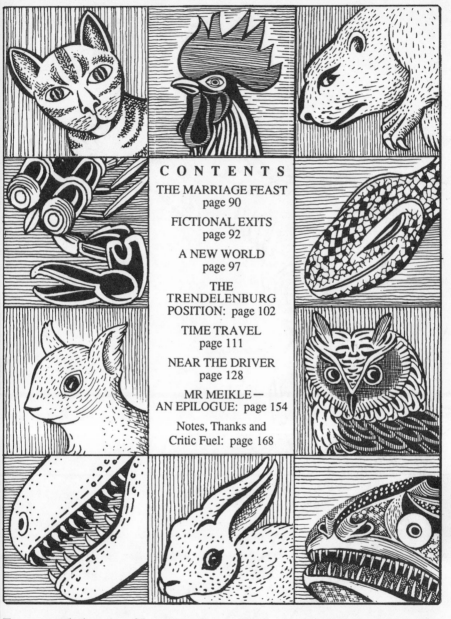

CONTENTS

I would spoil my book by shortening it,
spoil the title if I made it true.

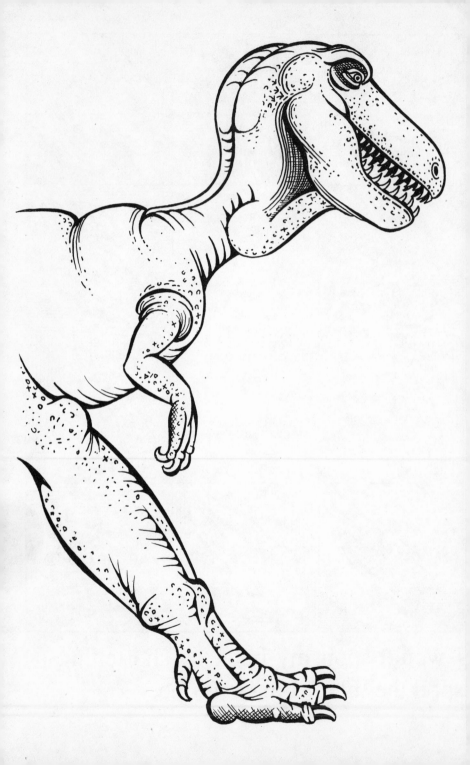

GETTING STARTED – A PROLOGUE

CALL ME ISHMAEL. Jesus wept. Reader, I married him. Pithiness prevents flow.

I remember the whole beginning as a succession of flights and drops, a little see-saw of the right throbs and the wrong. Far too vague.

I am the descendant of a race whose stolid unimaginative decency has, at all times, rendered them the dependable tools of others; yet from my earliest infancy I grew self-willed, addicted to the wildest caprices, a prey to the most ungovernable passions until bound and weary I thought best to sulk upon my mother's breast. Too romantic.

A man stood upon a railway bridge in Northern Alabama, looking down into the swift waters twenty feet below. The man's hands were behind his back, the wrists bound with a cord. That's the style for me.

EIGHT MEN DUG a trench beside a muddy crossroads, and the mud made two remember Italy where they had fought in a recent war. These two had not known each other in Italy, but both had seen a dead German who lay at a crossroads near Naples, though one thought it was perhaps nearer Pisa. They discussed the matter when the gang paused for a smoke.

"Not Pisa, no, Pisa was miles away," said one, "Naples was the place. He was a handsome big fella. We called him Siegfried."

"Our lot called him Adolf, because of the fuckin moustache," said the other, "He wasnae handsome for fuckin long."

"I don't remember a moustache, but you're right, he wasnae handsome for long. He went all white and puffy and swole up like a balloon – I think only his uniform stopped him bursting. The heavy traffic must have kept the rats away. Every time we went that road I hoped to God someone had shifted him but no, there he always was, more horrible than ever. Because eventually a truck ran over him and burst him up properly. Do you mind that?"

"I mind it fuckin fine."

"Every time we went that road we would say, 'I wonder how old Siegfried's doing,' and look out for him, and there was always something to see, though at last it was only the bones of a foot or a bit of rag with a button on it."

There was a silence. The older navvies thought about death and the youngest about a motorcycle he wanted to buy. He was known for being the youngest of them and fond of motorcycles. Everybody in the gang was known for something. Mick the ganger was known for being Irish and saying queer things in a solemn voice. One navvy was known for being a Highlander, one for having a hangover every morning, one for being newly married. One of the ex-army men was known for his war stories, the other for his fucking adjectives. One of them was a communist who thought *The Ragged Trousered Philanthropists* a better book than the Bible and kept trying to lend it; but schooling had given most of them a disgust of books. Only Old Joe borrowed it and he said it was a bit out of date. The communist wanted to argue the point but Old Joe was known for being silent as well as old. The youngest navvy liked working with these folk though he hardly ever listened to what they said. Too many of them wanted his attention. They remembered, or thought they remembered, when they too had been just out of school, sixteen and good-looking, happy because their developing muscles could still enjoy the strain of working overtime, happy because it was great to earn a wage as big as their fathers earned. The worst paid workers reach the peak of their earning power early in life.

"The Signoras!" announced the story teller suddenly, "The Signorinas! They were something else. Am I right? Am I wrong?"

"Aye, the fuckin Signoras were somethin fuckin else," said the other ex-army man. With both hands he shaped a huge bosom on the air before his chest.

"I'll give you a bit of advice Ian," the story-teller told the youngest navvy, "If you ever go to Italy take a few tins of bully beef in your suitcase. There is nothing, I'm telling you nothing you won't get from the Italian Signorinas in return for a can of bully beef."

"That advice may be slightly out of date," said Mick the ganger.

"You're sticking up for the Tally women because they're Papes and so are you, ye fuckin Fenian Irish Papal prick ye," said one of the ex-army men pleasantly.

"He's right, of course," the ganger told the youngest navvy, "I am a Papal Fenian. But if these warriors ever return to Italy they may find the ladies less welcoming now the babies have stopped starving."

He nipped his cigarette, stuck it under his cap brim above the right ear and lifted his pick. The gang began digging again.

Though their work was defined as unskilled by the Department of Labour they worked skilfully in couples, one breaking the ground with a pick, the other shovelling loose earth and stones from under his partner's feet and flinging it clear. At the front end Mick the ganger set a steady pace for all of them. The youngest navvy was inclined to go too fast, so Mick had paired him with Old Joe who was nearly sixty, but still worked well by pacing himself carefully. The two ex-army men were liable to slow down if paired together, so Mick always paired one of them with himself. The gang belonged to a workforce of labourers, brickies, joiners, plumbers, slaters, electricians, painters, drivers, foremen and site clerks who were enlarging a city by turning a hillside into a housing estate. During the recent war (which had ended seven years before but still seemed recent to all who remembered it) the government had promised there would be no return to unemployment afterward, and every family would eventually have a house with a lavatory and bath inside. The nation's taxes were now being spent on houses as well as armed forces, motorways, public health et cetera, so public housing was now profitable. Bankers and brokers put money into firms making homes for the class of folk who laboured to build them. To make these fast and cheaply standards of spaciousness and craftsmanship were lowered, makeshifts were used which had been developed during the war. Concrete replaced stonework. Doors were light wooden frames with a hardboard sheet nailed to each side. Inner walls were frames surfaced with plasterboard that dented if a door-knob swung hard against it. A tall man could press his fingers to the ceilings without standing on tiptoe. But every house had a hot water system, a bath and flush lavatory, and nearly everyone was employed. There was so much work that firms advertised for workers overseas and natives of the kingdom were paid extra to work at week-ends and during public holidays. In the building industry the lowest paid were proudest of what they earned by overtime work so most of this gang worked a six-day week. A labourer who refused overtime was not exactly scorned as a weakling, but thought a poor specimen of his calling. Recently married men were notoriously poor specimens, but seldom for more than a fortnight.

A heavily built man called McIvor approached the trench and stood for a while watching the gang with a dour, slightly menacing stare which was a tool of his trade. When his presence was noticed by the ganger, McIvor beckoned him by jerking his head a fraction to the side. Mick laid his pick carefully down, dried his sweating face with a handkerchief, muttered, "No slacking, men, while I confabulate with our commanding officer," and climbed out of the trench. He did not confabulate. He listened to McIvor, stroked his chin then shouted, "Ian! Over here a minute!"

The youngest navvy, surprised, dropped his spade, leapt from the trench and hurried to them. McIvor said to him, "Do you want some overtime? Sunday afternoons, one to five."

"Sure."

"It's gardening work but not skilled weeding, cutting grass, that sort of thing. It's at the house of Mr Stoddart, the boss. He'll give the orders. The rate is the usual double time. You get the money in your weekly pay packet."

"I thought Old Joe did that job."

"He does, but the boss says Joe needs help now. What do you say? Yes or no?"

"Aye. Sure," said the youngest navvy.

"Then I'll give you a word of advice. Mick here has pointed you out as a good worker so you'd better be, because the boss has a sharp eye for slackers – comes down on them like a ton of bricks. He also has a long memory, and a long arm. If you don't do right by Mr Stoddart you won't just get yourself in the shit, you'll make trouble for Mick here who recommended you. Right, Mick?"

"Don't put the fear of death into the boy," said the ganger, "Ian will do fine."

In the bothy where the navvies had their lunch an ex-army man said loudly and cheerfully, "I see the fuckin Catholics are stickin to-fuckin-gether as per fuckin usual."

"Could that be a hostile remark?" the ganger asked Ian, "Do you think the foul-mouthed warrior is talking about us?"

"Fuckin right I'm talking about yous! You could have gave the fuckin job to a fuckin family man like me with fuckin weans to feed but no, you give it to a fuckin co-religionist who's a fuckin wean himself."

"I'm not a Catholic!" said the youngest navvy, astonished.

"Well how do you come to be so fuckin thick with Mick the Papal prick here?"

"I recommended the infant of the gang for three reasons," said the ganger, "One, he is a bloody hard worker who gets on well with Old Joe. Two, some family men enjoy Sunday at home. Three, if one of us starts working around the boss's house he'll get the name of being a boss's man, which is good for nobody's social life, but Ian is too young to be thought that, just as Joe is too old."

"Blethers!" said the communist, "You are the boss's man here, like every ganger. You're no as bad as bastarding McIvor, but he comes to you for advice."

"Jesus Mary and Joseph!" cried Mick to the youngest navvy, "For the love of God get out of this and apprentice yourself to a decent trade! Go up to the joiners' bothy and talk to Cameron – they're wanting apprentice joiners."

"I'm not a Catholic, I've never been a Catholic," said the youngest navvy, looking around the others in the bothy with a hurt, alarmed and pleading expression. The Highlander (who was also suspected of being Catholic because he came from Barra, and someone had said everyone from that island were Catholics) said, "You are absolved – go in peace," which caused general amusement.

"Did you hear me Ian?" said the ganger sharply, "I told you to get out of this into a decent trade."

"I might, when I've bought my Honda," said the youngest navvy thoughtfully. He saw the sense in the ganger's advice. A time-served tradesman was better paid and had more choices of work than a labourer, but during the apprentice years the wage would be a lot less.

"Why did a clever fella like you never serve your time as a tradesman, Mick?" asked the communist.

"Because at sixteen I was a fool, like every one of us here, especially that silly infant. I never wanted a motorbike, I wanted a woman. So here I am, ten years later, at the peak of my profession. I've a wife and five children and a job paying me a bit more than the rest of you in return for taking a lot of lip from a foul-mouthed warrior and from a worshipper of Holy Joe Stalin."

"You havenae reached the peak yet Mick," said the communist, "In a year or three they'll give you McIvor's job."

"No, I'll never be a foreman," said the ganger sombrely, "The wages would be welcome, but not the loneliness. Our dirty tongued Orange friend will get that job – he enjoys being socially obnoxious."

The foreman had given the youngest navvy a slip of paper on which was written *89 Balmoral Road, Pollokshields*, and the route of a bus that would take him past there, and the heavily underlined words *1 a.m. on the dot*. The boy's ignorance of the district got him to the boss's house seven minutes late and gasping for breath. He lived with his parents on a busy thoroughfare between tenements whose numbers ran into thousands. When the bus entered Balmoral Road he saw number 3 on a pillar by a gate and leapt off at the next stop, sure that 89 must be nearby. He was wrong. After walking fast for what seemed ten minutes he passed another bus stop opposite a

gate pillar numbered 43, and broke into a jog-trot.
The sidewalk was a gravel path with stone kerb
instead of a pavement, the road was as wide and
straight as the one where he lived, but seemed
wider because of the great gardens on each side.
Some had lawns with flower-beds behind hedges,
some shrubberies and trees behind high walls,
both sorts had driveways leading up to houses
which seemed as big as castles. All of well-cut
stone, several imitated castles by having turrets,
towers and oriel windows crowned with
battlements. Signboards at two or three entrances
indicated nursing homes, but names carved on
gate pillars (Beech Grove, Trafalgar, Victoria
Lodge) suggested most houses were private, and
so did curtains and ornaments in the windows. Yet
all had several rooms big enough to hold the
complete two-room flat where he lived with his
parents, or one of the three-room-and-kitchen flats
being built on the site where he laboured. But the
queerest thing about this district was the absence
of people. After the back of the bus dwindled to
an orange speck in the distance, then vanished, the
only moving things he saw were a few birds in the
sky and what must have been a cat crossing the
road a quarter mile ahead. His brain was baffled
by no sight or sign of buildings he thought always
went with houses: shops, a post-office, school or
church. Down the long length of the road he could
not even see a parked car or telephone box. The
place was a desert. How could people live here?

Where did they buy their food and meet each other? Seeing number 75 on another gate pillar he broke into an almost panic-stricken run.

Number 89 was not the biggest house he had seen but still impressive. On rising ground at a corner, it was called The Gables and had a lot of them. The front garden was terraced with bright beds of rose bushes which must have been recently tended by a professional gardener. A low, new brick wall in front hid none of this. The young navvy hurried up a drive of clean granite chips which scrunched so loudly underfoot that he wanted to walk on the trim grass verge, but feared his boots would dent it. Fearful of the wide white steps up to the large front door he went crunching round the side to find a more inviting entrance, and discovered Old Joe building a rockery in the angle of two gables.

"Hullo Joe. Am I late? Is he angry?"

"I'm your gaffer today so don't worry. Fetch ower yon barrow and follow me."

Behind the house was a kitchen garden, a rhododendron shrubbery and a muddy entry from a back lane. Near the entry lay a pile of small boulders and a mound of earth with a spade in it. Joe said, "Bring me a load of the rocks then a load of the earth and keep going till I tell ye different. And while we're away from the house I don't mind telling you ye're on probation."

"What's that supposed to mean?"

"He watches us. He's seen you already."
"How? Why do ye think that?"
"You'll know why when he talks to ye later."

As they worked on the rockery the young navvy looked cautiously about and gradually grew sure they were the only folk in the garden. The walls of the house where they worked were blank, apart from a wee high-up window that probably ventilated a lavatory. When he wheeled the barrow to the back entry he was in view of larger windows. He kept bringing boulders and earth to Joe who worked kneeling and sometimes said, "Put that there, son," or "Give a shovelful here." Nearly an hour passed then Joe sighed, stood slowly up, straightened his shoulders and said, "Five minutes."

"I'll just get another load," said the young navvy, lifting the shafts of the barrow. He was uneasily aware of the black little lavatory window above and behind him.

"We're entitled to five minute spells," said Old Joe quietly, "We need them."

"I don't need them. And I was late, you werenae." He went off with the barrow, loaded it and found Joe working when he returned. An hour later a gaunt, smartly dressed lady looked round a corner, called, "Your tea is in the tool-shed," then vanished behind the corner.

"Was that his wife?" asked the young navvy.

"His housekeeper. Are you working through the

tea-break too?"

The young navvy blushed.

The tool-shed, like the garage, was part of a big newly built outhouse, and windowless, and had a roller shutter door facing the back entry. It smelt of cement, timber and petrol; had shelves and racks of every modern gardening and construction tool, all shiningly new; also a workbench with two mugs of tea and a plate of chocolate biscuits on it; also a motorcycle leaning negligently against a wall, though there were blocks for standing it upright.

"A Honda!" whispered the young navvy, going straight to it and hunkering down so that his eyes were less than a foot from the surface of the thing he worshipped, "Whose is this?"

"The boss's son's."

"But he hasnae been using it," said the young navvy indignantly, noting flat tyres, dust on seat and metal, dust on a footpump and kit of keys and spanners strewn near the front wheel. What should be shining chromium was dull, with rust spots.

"He's got better things to think of," said Joe after swallowing a mouthful of tea, "He's a student at the Uni."

"Why does he no sell it?"

"Sentimental reasons. His da gave it him as a present, and he doesnae need the money."

The young navvy puffed out his cheeks and blew to convey astonishment, then went over to the bench. Since they were not in sight or earshot of anyone he said, "What's the boss like?"

"Bossy."

"Come on Joe! There's good and bad bosses. What sort is he?"

"Middling to average. You'll soon see."

Ten minutes later they returned to the garden and worked for over an hour before Joe said, "Five minutes," and straightened his back, and surveyed his work with a critical eye. The young navvy paused and looked too. He could see the rocks were well-balanced and not likely to sink under heavy rains, but the impending presence of the unseen Stoddart (maybe the biggest and bossiest boss he would ever meet) made him restless. After a minute he said, "I'll just get us another load," and went off with the barrow.

Half an hour later the rockery was complete. As they stood looking at it the young navvy suddenly noticed there were three of them and for a moment felt he had met the third man before. He was a massive man with a watchful, impassive face, clean white open-necked shirt, finely creased flannel slacks and white canvas sports shoes. At last the stranger, still looking at the rockery, said, "Seven minutes late. Why?"

"I got off at the wrong stop – I didnae know the street was so long."

"Makes sense. What's your name youngster?"

"Ian Maxwell."

"Apart from the lateness (which will not be docked from your wages) you've done well today, Ian. You too Joe. A very decent rockery. The gardener can start planting tomorrow. But the day's work is not yet done as Joe knows, but perhaps as you do not know, Ian. Because now the barrow, spade, fork, trowel go back to the tool-shed and are cleaned – cleaned thoroughly. There's a drain in the floor and a wall-tap with a hose attached. Use them! I don't want to find any wee crumbs of dirt between the tyre and the hub of that barrow. A neglected tool is a wasted tool. What you'd better know from the start Ian (if you and me are going to get on together) is that I am not gentry. I'm from the same folk you are from, so I know what you are liable to do and not do. But do right by me and I'll do right by you. Understood?"

The young navvy stared, hypnotized by the dour impassive face now turned to him. Suddenly it changed. The eyes stayed watchful but the mouth widened into what the young navvy supposed was a smile, so he nodded. The big man patted him on the shoulder and walked away.

The navvies went to the tool-shed and cleaned the tools in silence. The youngest was depressed, though he did not know why. When they had returned the tools to their places (which were easy to see, because there were three of everything so a gap in the ranks was as obvious as a missing tooth) the young navvy said, "Do we just leave now?"

"No. We wait for the inspection."

They did not wait long. There was a rattling of at least two locks then an inner door opened and Stoddart came through carrying a tray with two glasses, a whisky bottle and a jug of water. His inspection was a quick sideways glance toward the tool-racks before he said, "How old are you, Ian?"

"Nearly seventeen."

"Too young for whisky. I'm not going to teach you bad habits. But Joe and me haven't had our ne'erday yet. A bad thing, me forgetting old customs. A large one, Joe? Macallan's Glenlivet Malt?"

"Thanks, aye"

"Water?"

"No thanks."

"Quite right, better without ... Good stuff Joe?"

"Aye."

"How's the old back, the old lumbago, Joe?"

"No bad, considering."

"Aye, but age gets us all in the end – even me. I'm not as young as I was. We have to learn to take things easy, Joe."

"Aye," said Joe, and emptied the glass straight down his throat.

"God, that went fast!" said Stoddart, "Another one, Joe?"

"Goodnight," said Joe, and walked out.

"Goodnight Joe, and goodnight to you Ian. See you next week on the dot of one youngster. Joe will be taking a bit of a rest. Right?"

"Thanks," said the young navvy, and hurried after Joe wondering why he had said thanks instead of goodnight when he had been given nothing, had not even been paid yet for his labour.

The young navvy overtook Joe walking into the back lane and said, "Are you no going for a bus, Joe?"

"No. This is a shortcut."

"Can I come with you?" asked the young navvy, wondering why he was asking. Joe said nothing. They walked beside each other in a lane with a brick wall on one side, a railway embankment on the other. It could have been in the depths of the country. Grass, daisies and clover grew between two parallel paths made by car wheels and the verges were thick with dandelions, dockens, thistles, burdock. Branches from trees in the gardens behind the wall hung overhead. From the embankment hawthorns and brambles stuck thorny, leafy shoots between the sagging wires of a fence. The old and young navvy walked side by side in silence, each on one of the parallel tracks. The young one felt Joe was angry, feared it had to do with him, tried to think of something to say.

And at last said, "When the boss turned up beside us there I thought he was McIvor at first."

Joe said nothing.

"Don't you think he's a bit like McIvor, Joe?"

"Of course he's like McIvor. McIvor is a foreman. Stoddart is the foreman's foreman – the gaffer's gaffer. Of course he's like McIvor."

"But he's cheerier than McIvor – he calls ye by your first name. Have you had drinks with him before, Joe?"

"That was the first and last."

"The last? Why the last?"

"Because you've done for me."

"What do you mean?" asked the young navvy, suddenly seeing exactly what the old one meant but confused by two amazements: amazement that the boss preferred him to Joe, amazement at the unfairness and speed of the result. Together these amazements stopped him feeling very happy or very angry. But he liked Joe so the unfairness puzzled him.

"Are you sure he doesnae ever want ye back Joe? I never heard him say so."

"Then you need your ears washed."

"But that cannae be right, Joe! I've got more muscle than you but I havenae the head yet – the skill. That's why Mick keeps pairing us. If I'm working just by myself I won't do so much because I'll need to keep stopping to think."

"Too true!" said Joe, "Stoddart is stupider than he knows, but he's a boss so nobody can put him right. In a week or two when he sees you arenae doing as well as you did today he'll think you've started slacking so give you the heave and get in someone else. Or maybe no! If ye arrive ten minutes early every day, and work your guts out till he tells ye to stop, and if you take a five minutes tea-break or none at all when the housekeeper forgets ye – well, if ye sweat enough at showing you're a boss's man he'll maybe keep ye."

Joe climbed over the fence and went up the embankment by a path slanting through willow herb and the young navvy followed, his confused feelings tinged by distress. Joe led him across three sets of railway lines to a gap in a fence of upright railway sleepers. They were now in a broad, unpeopled street between old warehouses. "What should I do Joe?" asked the youngest navvy. He was not answered, so said it again. After a long silence Joe suddenly said, "Get out of this into civil engineering, son. No bastard can own you in civil engineering because ye travel all over. Highland power stations, motorways in the Midlands, reservoirs in Wales – if ye tire of one job ye just collect your jotters and wages, clear out the same day and go to another. Naebody minds. No questions asked. And the money, the overtime is phenomenal. Once at Loch Sloy I worked a forty-eight hour stint – forty-eight hours with the usual breaks of course, but I was on the job the whole time without one wink of sleep. Someone bet me I couldnae but I could and I did. Civil engineering is the life, son, for folk like you and me. Of course most of the money goes on booze and betting, there's nothing much else to do with it. Some keep a wife and weans on the money but why bother? Ye only get to see them one week in six maybe. Family life is a con, a bloody imposition. Not that I'm advocating prostitutes! Keep clear of all women, son, is my advice to you: if they don't give you weans they'll give you some other disease. Chuck Stoddart and go into civil engineering. It's the only life for a man while he has his strength. That's what I did and I've never regretted it."

Joe seldom said more than one sentence at a time so the young navvy brooded over this speech. Booze, betting and prostitutes did not attract him. He wanted to hurl himself through the air toward any target he chose, going faster than a mile a minute with maybe a girl clinging on a pillion behind. But a good bike cost nearly £400. After paying his people two thirds of his weekly earnings in return for the home and services he had enjoyed since infancy, about £4 remained which (despite his intentions of saving £3 a week) seemed always to get eaten up by tram, café, cinema, dancehall, football, haircut and clothes expenses – he had begun to like dressing well on his few nights out. But if he worked on a big civil engineering job in the Highlands, and did all the twelve or sixteen hour shifts his strength allowed, and slept and ate cheaply in a workers' hostel, and paid his people a few shillings a week till he felt like returning, he might earn enough to buy a good bike in less than a year. Then the neglected Honda in the boss's tool-shed came to mind, and Stoddart's words A neglected tool is a wasted tool. He decided that next Sunday, perhaps during the tea-break, he would set the Honda in its blocks, clean it and tidy away the tools. Stoddart would certainly notice this and say something during the five o'clock inspection, and the young navvy had a feeling this might lead to something useful. He did not know what, but found the prospect oddly exciting, though he still felt sorry for Joe.

While he pondered these things they crossed a bridge over a railway cutting and came to Kilmarnock Road. It was a busy road with the railway on one side and on the other wee shops and pubs on the ground floors of ordinary tenements. The young navvy knew this road well. He travelled it by tramcar six days a week from his home to the building site and back. He was perplexed to find it so near the foreign, almost secret city of huge rich houses. A few blocks away he noticed a sign of a station where a subway train would take him home in time for the usual family tea. His distress vanished. He said, "I don't think my ma or da would like me going off to civil engineering just yet, Joe, but I'll take a crack at it one day. Thanks for the tip. See you the morrow."

Joe nodded and they separated.

THIS thirty-year-old college lecturer is big, stout, handsome, with the innocent baby face of a man used to being served by women, the sulky underlip of one who has never been served as much as he wants. It is Sunday afternoon. He compares the dial of his wristwatch with that of a small ornate clock under a glass dome on his mantelpiece. Both indicate 2.49. He sighs and looks critically round the apartment like a mechanic surveying a machine that has stopped working for him. Walls are pale grey, woodwork white, the moss-green fitted carpet harmonizes (not too obviously) with his immaculate dark-green sweater. A large low bed lacks foot and headboard, has big blue cushions strewn on it, and derives an air of invitation from a nearby coffee table on which lie a board supporting cold roast chicken, oatcakes, pat of butter, knife, salt-cellar; a salver of apples, peaches, grapes; a dish of small bright cakes and sweets. A few stones in the marble fireplace look nothing like coal, but bright flames among them give the air warmth which would make undressing easy, without making clothed people sweat. Through an oriel window a view of sunlit treetops can be blotted out (when wished) by smoothly running floor-length curtains, curtains with the light tone of his finely creased flannel trousers. Yet he sighs again, not feeling truly at home. Maybe an apple will help. He goes determinedly to the table but hesitates to disturb his arrangement of the fruit. A bell chimes softly. Smiling with relief he leaves the room, crosses a small lobby, opens the front door and says, "Vlasta."

A bitterly sobbing woman runs in past him. He looks out into the corridor, sees nobody else, closes the door.

Returning to the main room he stands watching the woman and thoughtfully rubbing his chin. She crouches on an easy chair, handbag on lap, sobbing into handkerchief. She is bony and fortyish with wild black hair flowing over the shoulders of her fur coat, a long black skirt and histrionic earrings. The sobs lessen. He tiptoes to

the coffee table, lifts and places it softly near her
right elbow, selects an apple and sits on a chaise-longue facing her. Cautiously he bites the apple. Her sobbing stops. She removes mirror from handbag and blots off tears, taking care not to damage make-up. He says softly, "I'm glad you came. Eat something. It sometimes helps."
She says hoarsely, "You are always so sweet to me, Alan."
She restores mirror and hanky to handbag, tears a wing from the chicken, bites, swallows and says, "Half an hour ago I threw out Arnold. He did not want to go. I had to call the police. He was drunk and violent. He cracked my tortoise, Alan."
"You were right to call the police."
"He was sweet to begin with – just like you. And then he went bad on me. Eventually they all go bad on me – except you."
She bites and swallows more chicken.

Then looks around and says, "Are you expecting someone?"
He smiles sadly, says, "Expecting someone? I only wish I was."
"But this food! ... And the room. You did not always keep it so spick and span."
"I do nowadays. I've become a real old woman since you left me, Vlasta, hoovering the carpet, dusting the clock – I've even grown cranky about food. I don't eat regular meals any longer. I keep plates of fruit and cold chicken beside me and have

a nibble whenever I feel like it."

"How odd! But have you no little girlfriend? No mistress?"

With a harsh laugh Alan throws the apple core into a brass coal-scuttle he uses as a waste basket and says, "None! None! I know plenty of women. I've invited some of them up here, and they've come. A few stayed the night. But (I don't know why) they all bored me. After you they were all so insipid."

"I knew it!" cries Vlasta exultantly, "Yes I knew it! When I left you I told myself, You are destroying this man. You have taught him all he knows and now that you leave him his confidence will vanish also. In fact you are castrating him! But I had to do it. You were sweet but ... oh so deadly dull. No imagination. And so I had to leave."

"It was agony," he assures her.

"I knew. I was sorry for you but I needed excitement. I will take my coat off, this room is far too warm, how can you bear it?"

She stands and flings her chicken bone into the scuttle. But Alan has risen first. Slipping behind her he helps remove the coat murmuring, "Perhaps you'll remove more before you leave."

"What a fool you are Alan – you still know nothing about women. It was four years ago, not last week we ceased to be lovers. I came here for peace, not erotic excitement. In the last three hours I have had more excitement than many of the bourgeoisie experience in a lifetime."

"Sorry!" murmurs Alan, and carries coat to bed.
He lays it there then sits on bedfoot, right elbow
on knee, right hand supporting chin like Rodin's
Thinker.

"I am a dreadful woman, I destroy men!" says
Vlasta, yawning and stretching her arms, "Arnold
kept shouting that while the policemen dragged
him away."

"Please sit beside me. I'm very lonely."

She sits beside him saying, "Think of Mick
McTeague, old before his time and drinking like
a fish."

"He was a sixty-year-old alcoholic when you first
met him."

"He's worse now. Last week I saw Angus pushing
his baby in a pram in the park, a slave to a woman
too foolish to understand him."

"He seems perfectly happy to me," says Alan,
looking at her, "We play snooker sometimes."

She laughs aloud at his naivety.

"Oh Alan have you forgotten everything I taught
you? Beneath the calmest of lives all sorts of
dreadful things are happening: spiritual rapes,
murders, incests, tortures, suicides. And the
calmer the surface the worse what is hidden
beneath."

Her perfume fills his nostrils, her body is an inch
away, with real excitement he declares, "I love the
way you turn life into an adventure, an exciting,
idiotic adventure."

"IDIOTIC?" she cries, glaring.

"No no no no!" he explains hastily, "That was a slip of the tongue, a device by which my conventional bourgeois hypocricy attempted to defend itself."

"Hm!" she says, only slightly placated, "I see you remember some of the things I taught you."

She sits beside him again, yawns and says, "Ahoo I am very tired. It is exhausting work, explaining life to thick policemen."

She lies back on the bed with her face upward and eyes closed.

A minute passes in silence. He stealthily pulls off his shoes, lies beside her and unfastens the top button of her blouse. Without opening her eyes she says in a small voice, "I told you I was in no mood."

"Sorry."

He sighs and resumes the Rodin's Thinker pose. After a while she says lazily, "I love you for being so easily discouraged."

He looks hopefully round. Her eyes are open, she is smiling, then laughing and sitting up and embracing him.

"Oh Alan, I can refuse you nothing! You are like an ugly old comfortable sofa I must always fall back upon."

"Always at your service!" he assures her. They stand, he pulls off his sweater, she starts removing her blouse and a bell chimes.

The doorbell chimes. He stands as if
paralysed and whispers, "Fuck."
She cries, "You WERE expecting someone!"
"No. Nonsense. Ignore it. Please speak more
quietly Vlasta!"
The bell chimes.
"Do you tell me you do not know who is there?"
"I swear it."
"Then go to the door and send them away," cries
Vlasta, rapidly fastening her blouse, "Or I will!"
The bell chimes. She strides to the lobby, he
dodges before her and stands with his back to the
front door hissing, "Be sensible Vlasta."
"Open that door or I will scream!"
Through clenched teeth he mutters, "Listen! This
might be, just might be, a young woman I greatly
admire and respect. She must not be upset, you
hear? She must not be upset!"
The bell chimes. Vlasta smiles coolly, folds her
arms, says, "So open the door."

He does. A stout man wearing a raincoat and
trilby hat stands outside. He says, "Scottish
Power. Can I read your meter sir?"
"Yes," says Alan. He opens a cupboard (Vlasta
has strolled back to the main room) and the man
directs a torch beam on the dials of a squat black
box.
"Sorry I'm late Alan," says a small pretty girl of
perhaps eighteen who strolls in.
"Hullo," says Alan. She goes into the big room

and Alan hears her say brightly, "Hullo – my name is Lillian Piper."

He hears Vlasta say, "You are one of his students of course."

"Yes!"

"What a coward he is."

"In Australia," says the stout man writing figures on a pad, "All meters have dials which can be read from outside the main door. I wish we had that system here sir."

"Yes. Goodbye," says Alan shutting the stout man out. Then he sighs and joins the ladies.

Vlasta (grim faced, arms folded, legs astride) stands in the middle of the room. Lillian stands near the fire looking thoughtfully at the rumpled bed-cover and his sweater on the floor beside it.

"Lillian," says Alan, "This is Vlasta – Vlasta Tchernik, old friend I haven't seen for years. She called unexpectedly ten or twenty minutes ago."

"He was seducing me when the meter man called," explains Vlasta, "He had my blouse off."

"Is that true?" Lillian asks him.

"Yes."

"Oh Alan."

Lillian sits down on a chaise-longue, Alan on the easy chair. They seem equally depressed. Vlasta, glaring from one to the other, feels excluded, awaits an opening.

At last Alan tells Lillian, "I wish you had

come when you said you would. I'd given you up."

"I was only forty minutes late! I've been very
punctual till now."

"I know. So I thought . . . since you didn't even phone . . . that you'd suddenly tired of me."

"Why did you think that? We got on so well the last time we met . . . Didn't we?"

"Oh I enjoyed myself. But did you?"

"Of course! I told you so."

"Maybe you were just being polite. A lot of women are polite at those times. After I'd waited fifteen minutes I thought, She was being polite when she said she enjoyed herself last time. And after twenty minutes I thought, She's not coming. She's met someone more interesting."

Lillian stares at him.

"He has NO self-confidence!" cries Vlasta triumphantly, "He is a weakling, a coward, a liar, a cheat, and DULL! Oh so deadly dull."

"Nonsense," says Lillian, but without much force, "He says very clever things sometimes."

"Can you give me an example?"

Lillian thinks hard and eventually says, "We went a walk last Sunday and he said, The countryside looks very green today but I suppose that's what it's there for."

"He was quoting me," says Vlasta with satisfaction, "And I got it from a book."

"Were you quoting her?" Lillian asks Alan. He nods. She sighs then tells Vlasta that cleverness isn't important – that Alan says very sweet sincere things which matter a lot more.

"Oho!" cries Vlasta, inhaling deeply like a war-horse scenting blood, "This really interests me – tell me about these sweet sincere things."

She strides to the chaise-longue and sits beside Lillian.

"Would either of you like a glass of sherry?" asks Alan loudly. He has gone to the fireplace, unstoppered a heavy cut-glass decanter and now tilts it enquiringly above a row of frail glasses on the mantelpiece. The ladies ignore him. He fills a glass, swigs it, then fills and swigs a second. Vlasta says, "Tell me just one of his sweet tender remarks."

"I'd rather not," says Lillian shortly.

"Then I will tell one to you. Let me think . . . yes. When you get in bed together, does he stretch himself and say in a tone of oh such heartfelt gratitude Thank God I'm home again ?"

Lillian is too depressed to speak but nods once or twice. Vlasta notices Alan swallow a third sherry and says, "You are trying to give yourself Dutch courage."

"I'm trying to anaesthetize myself," he tells her sulkily. Lillian goes to him saying, "Give me the sherry Alan."

She reaches for the decanter. He gives it to her. She drops it to smash on the hearth tiles and says, "You don't deserve anaesthetic," and wanders away from him, clenching her hands and trying not to weep. He stares aghast saying, "Lillian!

Lillian!" then sighs, kneels, takes a brass-handled shovel and broom from a stand of fire-irons and starts sweeping up the mess.

But Vlasta is more impressed than he is. She cries, "That was magnificent! You are wonderful, little Lillian! People think I am very fierce and violent because I always tell the truth, but believe me I am too timid to smash furniture."
Lillian asks harshly, "What other sweet things did he say to you?"
"Stop!" cries Alan. He pitches broom, shovel, broken glass into the scuttle and says firmly, "Leave us, Vlasta, we're as miserable as you could want us to be."
He is head and neck taller than Lillian, half a head taller than Vlasta, and for the first time today his bulk suggests dignity. But Vlasta says, "I enjoy myself! I shall not leave," and answers his stare with a hard bright smile, so he says quietly to Lillian, "Lillian I have been stupid, very stupid. Maybe in a week or two you'll be able to forgive me, or even sooner, I hope so. I hope so. But this is an indecent situation. Please clear out before she hurts you any more."
"She didn't hurt me," says Lillian, "You did. And I have no intention of being hurt any more. Vlasta! Thank God I'm home again. What other things did he say?"
"I get no pleasure from this conversation!" says Alan loudly, "You two may, I do not. Vivisect me

all you like – behind my back. I'm going to my *mother's* house. Feel free to use the kitchen if you want a cup of tea. The front door will lock itself when you leave. Have a nice day."

By now he is in the lobby taking a coat from the cupboard. He hears Lillian say, "He's very house-proud, isn't he? How much do you think this cost?"

"Oh a great deal of money," says Vlasta. "Will you smash it too?"

Through the doorway he sees Lillian standing with her hand on the glass dome over his clock. He drops the coat and goes to her with arms outstretched like a fast sleepwalker saying, "Lillian, no! That has a Mudge pirouette triple escapement oh please please don't jar the movement!"

Lillian retreats from the clock but grabs a slender clay ornament from the top of a book-case. She holds it straight above her head like a flagstaff saying, "What about this?"

"That is a terracotta by Shanks!" cries Alan in an agony of dread, "By Archibald Shanks, for God's sake be careful Lillian!"

"Strange how much he cares about things being hurt and how little about feelings being hurt," says Vlasta. Alan tries to master the situation with college lecturer's logic.

"In the first place I haven't tried to hurt people's feelings, I've simply tried to, to, to enjoy myself. In the second place of course things are more

important than feelings. Everybody recovers from
hurt feelings, if they aren't children, but damage
a well-made clock or ceramic and a certain piece
of human labour and skill and talent leaves the
world for ever. Please Lillian – put that figurine
down."
"Smash it!" hisses Vlasta.

Lillian has never before had two adult people
so interested in what she will do next. It makes her
playful. She has also been slightly impressed by
the last part of Alan's speech. The figurine, though
too simplified to suggest a personality, is
obviously female. Lillian cradles it in her arms,
pats the head and says, "Don't worry little statue,
I won't hurt you if your owner acts like a sensible
boy and doesn't run away to his mummy
whenever life gets tough for him. Sit down Alan.
What were you going to say about him Vlasta?"
She sits beside Vlasta on the sofa. Alan, after a
pause, slumps down in the easy chair, notices the
chicken, wrenches off a leg and tries to comfort
himself by chewing it.
"Have you noticed," says Vlasta, "How he always
plans his seductions with food nearby? Obviously
sex and eating are very mixed up inside his brain.
I have not worked out what that means yet, but
something nasty anyway."
Alan stares haggardly at the bone in his hand then
lays it down.
"Then again," says Vlasta, "He is not a very

passionate lover physically."

"Isn't he?" asks Lillian, surprised.

"Oh I do not say that he gives us no pleasure but he depends upon words too much. He keeps whispering these little monologues, erotic fantasies, you know what I mean?" – Lillian nods; Alan sticks his fingers in his ears – "He can get you very excited by mixing this into his foreplay but when he nears the climax he just lies back and leaves all the work to the woman. Eventually this becomes dull. How long have you known him?"

"A fortnight."

Vlasta looks at Alan and shouts, "Take your fingers out of your ears!"

Lillian holds out the figurine by its feet at the angle of a Nazi salute. Vlasta shouts, "Remember the talent and skill which made this statue! Will you see them leave the world forever because you are ashamed of hearing a few simple facts?"

Alan withdraws fingers from ears and covers his face with them. The women contemplate him for a minute, then Vlasta says, "What monologues has he used on you?"

"The king and queen one."

"That is new to me."

"He pretends we are a king and queen making love on top of a tower in the sunlight. There is a little city below with red roofs and a harbour with sailing ships going in and out. The sailors on the sea and farmers on the hills round about can see us from miles away. They're very glad we're doing that."

"Very poetic! Yet the scene is strangely familiar
– Ah, I remember now! It is a picture in a book I lent him, Jung's *Psychology and Alchemy*. But have you never had to be Miss Blandish?"

Alan stands up looking dazed and walks, snapping fingers, to the bed, on which he flings himself flat with face pressed deep into coverlet. The women arise and follow him, Lillian with the figurine still cradled in her arms. They sit primly on the foot of the bed with Alan's heels between them.

"No," says Lillian, "I have never had to be Miss Blandish."

"He would have made you that eventually. *No Orchids for Miss Blandish* was a sadistic American thriller which made a great impression on him when he was ten or eleven. It is a pity Britain has no respectable state-inspected brothels, male adolescents here get initiated into sex through books and films which leave them with very strange ideas. Alan is such a milksop that I expected his intimate fantasies to be masochistic – no such luck! I had to be Miss Blandish while he raved like a madman in a phoney Chicago accent. Does that connect with his feelings for food? Yes of course! Too little breast feeding in infancy has made him an oral sadist. At the same time his clinging attitude to objects is a transference from the oral and anal retention syndrome."

Alan, without moving, emits a small but sincere

scream.

"End of round two," says Vlasta happily, "Enemy flat on canvas."

But Lillian is not happy. She lays the figurine carefully on the floor and says sadly, "You know, when he spoke to me at these times I used to feel so special . . ."

"And now you know you have been to bed with a second-hand record player."

Speaking with difficulty Alan turns his head sideways and says, "If I – sometimes – said the same thing to both of you – it was only because you both – sometimes – made me feel the same way."

"How many women have made you feel the same way?" demands Vlasta, then sees Lillian is sobbing. Vlasta places a hand on her shoulder and says hoarsely, "Yes weep, weep little Lillian. I wept when I came here. YOU have not wept yet!" she tells Alan accusingly.

"And I'm not going to," he declares, sitting up and wriggling down to the bed-foot on Lillian's side. He hesitates then says awkwardly, "Lillian, I haven't had time to tell you this before but I love you. I love you."

He looks at Vlasta and says, "I don't love you at all. Not one bit. But since you don't love me either I don't know why you're so keen to crush me."

"You deserve to be crushed, Alan," says Lillian in a sad remote voice. He wriggles close to her pleading: "I honestly don't think so! I've been selfish, greedy, stupid and I told Vlasta a lot of lies but I never tried to hurt anyone – not even for fun. My main fault was trying to please too many people at the same time, and believe me it would never have happened if only you had been punctual Lillian . . . "

In order to see her face he stands up and shatters the figurine under foot. The women also stand and look down at the fragments.

Slowly he kneels, lifts the two biggest fragments and holds them unbelievingly at eye-level. He places them carefully on the floor again, his mouth turning down sharply at the corners, then lies flat again on the bed. Lillian sits beside him, supporting herself with an arm across his body. She says sadly, "I'm sorry that happened, Alan."

"Are you sympathizing?" cries Vlasta scornfully.

"I'm afraid so. He's crying, you see."

"You do not think these tears are real?"

Lillian touches his cheek with a fingertip, licks the tip, touches the cheek again and holds out her finger to Vlasta saying, "Yes, they are. Taste one." Vlasta sits down too, presses Lillian's hand to her lips, keeps it there. Vlasta says, "What beautiful fingers you have – soft and small and shapely."

"Oh?"

"Yes. I'm more than a little butch, you know. How else could I have given myself to a thing like

THAT?"

But Lillian is tired of this game and pulls her fingers away.

And leans closer to Alan, lays her hand gently on his neck and murmurs, "I'm sure Archibald Shanks has made hundreds of little statues. You can always get another."

In a muffled voice he says, "'Snot just that. I've ruined everything between you and me, you and me."

Lillian says, "I don't hate you, Alan," and snuggles closer. Vlasta, watching them, feels excluded again, but knows anger and denunciation will exclude her even more. She also feels a softening toward Alan. Is it pity? No, it is certainly not pity, she has no pity for men and enjoys destroying them, especially smart manipulators like Alan. But when you have knocked such a man down, and don't want to go away and be lonely, what can you do but help set him up again, like a skittle?

"I too cannot exactly hate you Alan," she says, snuggling close to his other side. And he, with heartfelt gratitude, thanks God he is home again.

IN HER mid-twenties she does not move or dress attractively so only looks handsome when still, like now. She sprawls on floor, arms folded on seat of the easy chair she uses as desk. Pencil in hand, notepad under it, she studies open book propped against chairback: the one book in a room whose furnishings show only that the users are neither poor nor rich. This a room to lodge, not live in, unless your thoughts are often elsewhere. She frowns, writes a sentence, scores it out, frowns and writes another. A vertical crease between dark eyebrows is the only line on her face.

A door opens so she puts cushion over book

and notepad then sits back on heels, watching a man enter. Ten years older than she he wears good tweed overcoat and looks about in worried way muttering, "Keys. Forgot keys."

"There!" she says, pointing. He takes keys from top of sound-deck, returns toward door but pauses near her asking, "What did you hide under the cushion?"

"Nothing."

"Don't be silly."

"Why not look and see?"

"Thanks. I will."

He grasps cushion, hesitates, pleads: "Do you mind if I look?"

"Oh look look look!" she cries, standing up, "I can't stop you. It's your cushion. It's your room."

He moves cushion, lifts book and turns to the title page: *The Pursuit of the Millennium, a Study of Revolutionary Anarchism in the Middle Ages.*

"Very clever," he murmurs, and puts the book where he found it and settles on a sofa, hands clasped between knees. This depressed attitude angers her. Looking down on him she speaks with insulting distinctness. "Shall I tell you what's in the battered green suitcase under our bed? Sidney's *Arcadia*. Milton's *Paradise Lost*. Wordsworth's *Prelude*. And a heap of notes for a thesis on the British epic."

He sighs. She walks up and down then says, "You'd better hurry, you'll be late for the office."

"What office?" he asks, astonished.

"Wherever you work between nine and five."
"You know nothing about my life," he tells her
sharply, "Or have you been reading my letters?"
"Nobody writes to you."
"Good! When I go through that door each morning
I become a mystery. Maybe I don't need to work.
Maybe each morning I go to see my mistress. My
other mistress!"
"Then you'd better hurry or you'll be late for your
other mistress."
But he does not move.

She sits, tries to read her book, fails and puts
it down.
"Listen," she says in a softer voice, "I know men
hate clever women. I've known it since I was
twelve. But we've got on well together. Forget I'm
clever. I won't remind you."
"I'm not depressed because you're clever. I saw
you were deep from the moment we met. I'm
depressed because now I know what happens in
your head. Next time you frown I'll think, 'Damn!
She's worrying about her thesis.'"
"Why damn? Why will it upset you?"
"Because I'll feel obliged to say something
cheerful and reassuring."
"Do you really resent making ordinary, friendly
little remarks?"
"Yes."
"What a selfish attitude! Anyway, you couldn't
reassure me on my thesis. You're too ignorant."

He stares at her. She blushes and says, "Sorry. You've no books and I take books too seriously. You're probably as clever in your own way as I am, what do you do for a living?"

"I won't tell you."

"Why?"

"If you get to know me well you'll despise me."

"Why? Are you in advertising?"

"Certainly not. But familiarity breeds contempt."

"Not always."

"Yes always!"

She rises and walks about saying, "Our friendship has taken a steep turn for the worse in the last five minutes and it's not my fault."

He sighs then asks, "Were you ever married? Or (because it comes to the same thing) did you ever live long with someone?"

"No. But men have lived with me."

"Long?"

She thinks for a moment. Her last lover was an exciting young man whose work and opinions, good looks and quick speech sometimes got him asked onto television shows. He needed a lot of admiration and support. She had easily supplied these until she found he was also the lover of her close friend and flat-mate, then she noticed he was an emotional leech who had stopped her investigating Chaucer's debt to Langland for over a month. She says grimly, "Far too long."

"Then you know about lack of privacy. We start

sharing a bed and some rooms and meals which is fun at first, even convenient. Then we start sharing our thoughts and feelings and end in the shit. Have you noticed how cheerful I am in the morning?"

"I hear you singing in the lavatory."

"Does it annoy you?"

"A bit, but I can ignore it."

"You couldn't ignore it if you knew me well. My wife couldn't ignore it. If I sang or whistled or hummed she said I gave her a headache, so I crushed the melody in my bosom and became as miserable as she was. She was always very quiet in the morning. She got brighter in the evening, but not the early evening. I would come home from work and find her brooding. It was very strange. I knew that if I left her alone she would brighten eventually, but I couldn't. I found her black moods as much a pain as she found my cheerful ones. I would try nagging her into happiness: ask what was wrong then explain it was unimportant. Whenever we weren't equally bright or equally dull we nagged each other till we were equally miserable. All our conversations became wrestling bouts, like this one."

"This one?"

"This is our first real conversation and you've already called me selfish and ignorant. That nearly floored me."

"You started it."

"Yes guilty! Guilty! I'm like an alcoholic who can keep off his poison for weeks but after one sip can't stop till he's flat on his back. I've moaned to you about my marriage, I've started telling you about my bad habits, if you don't shut me up you'll soon know about my childhood, schooling, how I make my money . . ."

"Are you a hit-man for the Mafia?"

"Don't be silly. When I've cut myself into small pieces and handed them to you on a tray I'll get you to start talking."

She says shortly, "I don't like talking about myself."

"I know, but talk is the most infectious disease in the world. In a week or month or year we'll know each other thoroughly. You'll no longer be the lovely stranger who approached me in the singles bar, the mysterious she who shares my bed and breakfast. I'll have turned you into what we all are, basically – a pain in the arse with a case history behind it."

She laughs at that. Despite his words he is excited, almost cheerful, and watches her closely.

She sits down beside him, elbow on knee, chin on clenched fist. He lays an arm carefully round her shoulder but a slight shrug tells him she doesn't want that so he withdraws the arm. She is thinking that the trouble with his wife was probably sexual. In bed he leaves most of the initiatives to her. She does not mind this because though her last lover was more exciting he wanted applause for his performances and she

found this exhausting. Does the man beside her
think the last fortnight (the most restful and
productive fortnight of her life) has been romantic
adventure? Someone who can say I crushed the
melody in my bosom without irony is almost
certainly romantic. In a low voice she asks, "Do
you really think me what you said? Lovely –
mysterious?"

"I've managed it so far. You've been the greatest
thing in my life since wee Moody."

"Wee Moody?"

"She visited me when I'd done too many things in
too short a time. The doctor ordered a week of
complete rest so I sent the wife and kids away for
a holiday, unplugged the phone and stayed in bed
doing nothing but doze, watch the box and eat food
out of tins. The privacy was wonderful. On the
second day a cat ran in when I opened the door for
the milk. She was a neat little thing with a smooth
black coat but hungry, so I fed her. When I
returned to bed she came and curled in the hollow
behind my knees. I liked to stroke and pat her, she
was so graceful and . . . suave. When she wanted
out she patted the door with her paw and I let her
out, but she came in again next morning with the
milk. We kept company for nearly a week without
nagging or bullying each other. That was the
happiest time of my life, before I met you."

"Thank you. What became of her?"

"When the kids came home they adopted her –
they saw more of her than I did when I returned to

work. When the family left me they took her with them."

"A pity. You wouldn't need me if she had stayed."

"Nonsense! You're a woman with arms, legs et cetera, the whole female works. You're much nicer to me than wee Moody ever was."

She gets up and walks away. Strong feelings stop her speaking: amusement, pity, despair and anger. Anger is uppermost. She forces it down, hearing him say, "Our friendship is entering a new phase, isn't it?"

"No!" she tells him, turning, "It had better not. I agree with you about talk. Words do more harm than good if they aren't in a poem or play, and even plays have caused riots. Let's switch on the silence again. We came together because like most mammals we can't bear sleeping alone. You find me fascinating because you don't know me. I like living here because you're clean, gentle, undemanding, and don't interest me at all. Have I floored you?"

He nods, his mouth open and face paler than usual. She laughs and says, "Don't worry! I'll pick you up. I'm your mistress, not your cat. I've got arms." She lifts keys off the top of the sound-deck where he has dropped them again, puts them in his coat pocket, grasps his hands and pulls. He sighs and stands.

"Kiss me!" she says. He doesn't so she kisses him hard until his lips yield.

"Now go off to wherever you always go," she says, taking his arm and leading him to door, which she opens.

"But . . ." he says, pausing.

"Sh!" she whispers, pressing a finger to his lips, "I'll be here when you come back. Off you go."

He sighs, leaves. She shuts door, goes back to work.

YOU

GO TO WEDDING and reception afterward where, as usual, the bride's people and groom's people are strangers to each other. Tension. The groom's family are English, new here, trying not to show they are richer, feel superior to the bride's people, the Scots, the natives. Are in a small gang of bride's friends who know their best dresses will look cheap beside groom's sisters' and women friends' dresses, so dress deliberately down, making a uniform of jeans spectacularly ripped, tiny denim jackets showing midriffs and that we don't care how much money you lot like wasting on clothes. Bride's people are mortified. Feel sorry for them. Groom's people act amused, are perhaps not very, so to hell with them. This tall quite old man, nearly thirty – the well dressed kind who knows he is suave – keeps looking, not openly staring but giving quiet little humble yet slightly amused glances meaning hullo, I'm turned on, do you think we could? He is careful nobody else sees him giving the eye, but stays with his own posh English sort but only with the men until wonder (disappointed) is he gay? and (indignantly) does he think this get-up just comic? Forget him.

While putting food on a plate at the buffet find him close beside saying, "Can I help you to some of this?"
Thank him. Stand eating with back to the wall. So does he, saying thoughtfully, "Odd to be at my cousin's friend's wedding on the day my divorce comes through."

Look at him, surprised. He says, "I feel there's a lot of aggro going on under our jolly surfaces here. Do you?"
Agree.
"I don't think the tension is as Scottish-English as it looks. It's just bloody British. Whenever two British families come together one lot feel up, the other lot under. Guilt and resentment ensue and much silly jockeying. Even the Royals do it. I find these tensions boring. Do you?"
Agree.
"A woman of few words! I will shortly say

good-bye to the chiefs of my lot and the chiefs of your lot, then I will drive to the Albany and enjoy one of the best things your country makes: a Macallan Glenlivet malt. Have you been to the Albany?"

Have not.

"It's nice. I never stay there but I can always find a quiet comfortable bar there. I would like you to have a drink with me because (to be honest) this wedding on top of the divorce is making me feel lonely, and you look a nice person to talk to. And I promise not to say a word about my ex-wife and her wicked ways. I'd rather talk about something more pleasant and different. I'd love to talk about you if you can stand being probed a little by a disgusting Sassenach. Please don't say a word because I am now about to leave. In fifteen minutes I will be at the carpark, sitting hopefully inside a puce Reliant Scimitar. It's a silly car with a silly colour but perhaps it suits me. I can't tell you how I got it."

Ask if they let girls dressed like this into the Albany.

"Don't be so boringly British. But of course you're teasing me a little."

He leaves. He has done this before. Be careful.

The Albany has lounges upstairs for residents and their guests. He is neither, but the waiter serves him without question. Can people with his kind of voice and clothes go anywhere? But he does not try to make drunk.

"Do you prefer sweet or dry drinks?"

Prefer sweet.

"Good. I will buy you a very special cocktail which I'm sure you will enjoy if you sip it as slowly as I sip my Macallan, then we can have a coffee and I'll drive you home. Do you stay with your people?"

Live in a bedsit.

"Shared?"

Not shared.

"Good! Bad idea, sharing. It has destroyed many a friendship. Tell me about your people. Having no family of my own now I like hearing about other families."

Tell him about Dad, Mum, relations. He says thoughtfully, "It's nice to know there are still pockets of affection in the world."

Ask about his mum and dad.

"Aha! A touchy subject. I hardly ever see them, not even at Christmas. My father is nothing – nothing at all. He made a big killing in property and retired like a shot. My mother is merely supportive. They live in Minorca now. They were never very close."

Frown, puzzled. His words suggest bodiless people separating or propping each other after a ghostly massacre. Sigh. Silence. Here come the drinks. Sip. Enjoy this. Tell him so.

"Thought you'd like it. May I ask what you do for a living?"

Tell him.

"What's the firm like, the boss like?"

Tell him.

"What – if it's not an indelicate question – do they pay you?"

Tell him.

"How very mean! Can you live on a wage as low as that? We ought to do something about that. You would earn a lot more if you came to London. I know, because I'm in Systems Analysis which deals with your kind of firm, among others."

Don't be fooled by that one. Tell him everything costs more in London, especially the bedsits.

"Perfectly true, which is why London wages are higher too. But not everywhere. If you decide to come to London contact me first. And now I'll drive you home."

He does not try to touch on his way to the car or inside it, and stays in his seat on arriving. Not inviting himself in, he sits with hand on wheel smiling sideways. Think of saying thank you, good night, but instead ask him in. The loving is surprisingly good. He seems shy at first, not embarrassingly shy but charmingly shy, responds vigorously to hints, pleasuring first a long time with fingers and then with tongue, murmuring, "With this instrument I also make my money."

He pulls a condom on later saying, "I'm thinking

of your health. You don't know where I've been."
Feel safe with him. Have known nobody make
love as long as he does. Say so. He says, "We share
a talent for this. Let's do it again soon."
Yes do it again soon.

Of course his money smooths things. The
second night starts with a meal in the Shandon
Buttery costing more than a (not his) weekly wage,
on the third night another ditto at One Devonshire
Gardens, fourth night ditto in Central Hotel after
the disco. Dislike these meals, excepting the
starters and sweets. The main course is always too
fancy, too sauced, too spiced. Never say so. And
all the time he is kind, polite, funny, telling stories
about people whose faces are seen, names and
voices are heard on the news. His stories could
never be told on the news, make giggle they are
so stupid, blush they are so dirty, madden with
rage they are so unfair like the Duke of
Westminster and asbestosis. He seems to stand
outside the dark tank of an aquarium full of weird
cruel filthy comic fish, shining a light onto each
in turn, explaining with humour but also with a
touch of regret how greedy and wasteful they are.
He never explains how he knows them so well,
never talks about himself, but always about them,
the others. Maybe he learned about them as he
learned about Mum, Dad, the boss, by asking their
daughters and employees. If asked about himself
he gives a crisp reply in words that sound definite

but say nothing definite. Ask where he lives.

"London, half the year, but which half is problematic. I go where the firm needs me: Scotland just now."

Ask where he is staying in Glasgow.

"I'm a guest of people who called in my firm. It's one of the ways I learn things, so I run away to you whenever I can."

Ask about Systems Analysis.

"We unstick thing in businesses where things have got stuck. We also advise on mergers and acquisitions. It's all perfectly honest and above board. We're a registered company. Look us up in the directory if you don't believe me."

Ask what he does.

"At present I work mainly with newspapers – not for them, with them, because papers involve advertising, hence marketing. All very complicated."

Sigh, hating to be treated as an idiot. Ask if he works in accountancy, computer programming or time management.

"Yes, these are all part of it, but what I do best (and with considerable aplomb) is kick bums."

Ask if that means he sacks people. He chuckles and says, "Of course not, this is England! – I beg your pardon, Britain. Above a certain income level nobody gets sacked in Britain. My kicking simply shifts the bums to where they don't block things. If you want the details you should take a course in business management at London University, where I'll end up as a visiting lecturer if I'm not careful. My work pays a lot more than yours does, but in the long run is just as disgustingly boring. Perhaps more so."

Yet he is never short-tempered or depressed, always gentle, considerate, amusing, apologetic, letting no harshness or dulness appear, though it must exist. All folk have a nasty side which usually appears at the second or third meeting, if not the first. His appears on the fourth.

He calls at the bedsit between seven and eight and says with his usual humorous apologetic smile, "That dress won't do, I'm afraid."
Ask why.
"It looks cheap – doesn't suit you. Wear what you wore at the wedding. I insist."
Angry and cheapened, find no words to say no. While undressing, redressing he sits watching closely. Know you are exciting him. Grow slightly excited. Before dressing is finished he stands and comes to you, makes love at once fast. Don't enjoy it much. He sighs and says, "That was our best time yet, I suppose you noticed?"
Agree. Finish dressing. Resignedly display yourself.
"Perfect! You suit the Cinderella look. Let's be different tonight. Where would you go for fun if you didn't know me? A disco?"

Take him to a disco where he dances a bit

stiffly but well, considering his age. Like it that others (especially Tall Jenny) see him twisting before, around, beside in that well-cut suit, perfect shirt, tie flapping, fine blond hair flapping, and still the modest amused little smile.

"I'm whacked – need to stand still for a bit. But you're young – please go on dancing. I'm not a jealous type, I'll enjoy watching you dance."

Smile at him, pleased. Dance with a handsome gay in biker leathers. This is more fun as gay is better dancer and now have the pleasure of two partners, this Hunky Harry and him watching. Suddenly see him dancing nearby with Tall Jenny, most obviously attractive woman in the room. Are a little hurt but don't show it. Smile at them, twice, though they seem not to see. Never mind. Please go on dancing. Thanks mister, I will.

And suddenly enjoy it! For being with him (only notice this now) is a strain when not loving. Can never forget he is posh English, knows more about everything, is keeping a lot back so must think himself superior. Dance with boys who like dancing, like life without feeling superior. Have no shortage of partners, hooray for the ordinary! But while drinking a lime juice with a girl friend at the bar see him talking to Hunky Harry and laughing in a way that makes him look ordinary too, and much nicer. Stare at him, wanting him. He notices, stops laughing, comes over with his usual little smile and says, "Time to leave."

Are delighted. Truly delighted. Feared had lost him.

But both are quiet in the car as he drives to the Central Hotel, so something is wrong. Both are quiet because he is quiet, for it is always he who directs the talk or deals it out. Is he angry? Have done nothing wrong, unless it was wrong enjoying dancing with someone else. He is probably tired. Nearly midnight, now. Surprised the Central is still open.

Without a nod to the doorman he leads up broad shallow carpeted stairs to a lounge empty but for an elderly American-looking couple in a far corner. He tells a waiter, "This place seems quiet enough. Could you serve us a meal here?"
"Certainly sir, I'll fetch a menu."
"No need. This young lady wants nothing but a goodly selection of sandwiches and I will have **********." (French words.)
"I'm afraid the last is not available sir. The menu will show you what we can provide just now. We have . . ."
"Get me the manager."
"The manager is not available sir."
"Don't pretend to be stupid. You know I want whoever is in bloody charge here just now."
He has not lost his temper, has not raised his voice, but it has grown so distinct that the Americans look alarmed. The waiter leaves and returns with

another man in a black dinner-suit who says, "I'm sorry sir but the situation is this: the day chef retires at 10.45 and the night chef . . ."

"I did not come here for instruction in the mysteries of hotel management, I came because this used to be a good hotel, I happen to be hungry, and have a taste for **********, whose ingredients are now dormant in your kitchen. I mean to pay what it costs to have them expertly prepared. There is nothing to discuss. I am not going to explain, plead or bully you, so please don't use those tactics on me. Understood?"

He has not lost his temper. He looks at the head-waiter or under-manager or whoever this man is with a fixed half-smile containing no amusement or apology. The head-waiter or under-manager, his face paler than it was, says after a pause, "You are not a resident here sir?"

"No, nor ever likely to be. I promise this is the last time you will see me here, so do the wise thing and send up what I order?"

He says this softly, cooingly, teasingly, smiling almost sleepily as if at a joke the man before him is bound to share. The man before him, looking very pale, suddenly nods and walks away.

"One moment!" cries the Englishman – the head-waiter or under-manager turns – "I will have a bottle of ********** along with it."

Keep silent, though he watches sideways now. Was all that done to impress? Are chilled, embarrassed, disgusted, only glad the Americans

have stopped staring, are leaving. Sigh. He looks away. A long silence happens. He murmurs as if to himself, "Sometimes one has to be firm."
The barman pulls down a grille over the bar, locks it and leaves. He murmurs, "They'll probably take hours, just to be awkward."

The waiter brings the selection of sandwiches. Have no appetite but nibble half of one, then leave it. Later, from boredom, slowly finish it and then all the rest. Eventually the waiter serves him with a plate containing slips of meat half sunk in reddish gravy with a sweet heavy sickly smell. He looks hard at it, murmurs, "I don't think they've spat in it," and eats. After some forkfuls he says, "Yum yum. Well worth waiting for."

Are driven home, arrive about one thirty a.m. bored, tired, disliking him. In the silence when he stops the car and smiles sideways you want not to invite him in tonight but are about to do it as usual when he says, "Listen, I'm sorry about tonight. It started the best yet but ended badly. Nobody was to blame. Perhaps we need a rest from each other. Anyway, tomorrow night I have to see people, and the night after. Suppose we meet the night after that? You choose where."
Suggest lounge of the Grosvenor.
"Fine! Half seven, then."
Go upstairs yawning and wondering (without

much pain) if tomorrow night he will bed Tall Jenny or Hunky Harry, since obviously he can get anyone, anything he wants. Only wish had called off tomorrow before he did. But next day these ideas become a torment, why? Why care for someone so dislikeable? But he has usually been loving, gentle, pleasant, why dislike him? Is it bad to call out a hotel chef late at night if you pay the hotel enough to compensate for the extra trouble? When the bill came he glanced at it, grimaced slightly, wrote a cheque and gave it to the waiter without looking at him. And the waiter, glancing at it, became less stiff and expressionless, said, "Thank you very much sir," in a low voice, so he had been well tipped. One dull night after three lovely exciting nights is not bad, though he is far too obsessed with ragged jeans.

So here in the Grosvenor, ten minutes early, are dressed in a different high-heeled Cinderella way because that excites him, so slightly excited and hopeful too. Buy a lime juice, and for him a Macallan, the first thing you have ever bought him. Sit facing the door, whisky on table beside your lime juice and wait. And wait. And wait.

He arrives at half past eight, not smiling, and sits beside you muttering, "Detained. Unavoidable."
He sips the whisky, pulls a face, says, "What is this?"

Tell him.

"Are you sure?"

Tell him that was what you ordered.

"They've watered it."

Silence. Tell him something funny the boss did today. He nods twice and sighs. Silence. Ask him how his own work is going.

"Rottenly."

Say you are sorry.

"A woman of few words."

Ask why things have gone rottenly.

"I am sick of your unending probing into my personal affairs. If you have not already noticed I dislike that trait in women you are not just stupid, you are a cretin. A cretin may be good for three nights fucking in a filthy hole like Glasgow but three nights is the limit. Remember that."

He has not lost his temper. He stands and goes out, leaving the whisky almost untasted.

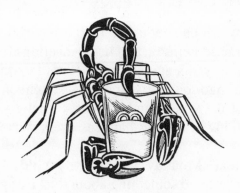

INTERNAL MEMORANDUM

TO : LUMLEY
FROM : LESLEY

The following will seem bad-tempered and in fact is. It says what I meant to raise at yesterday's meeting but my only chance came at the end when Phimister said, "Is there any further business?" and Henry Pitt (looking at me out of the corner of his eye) said, "No, I think that's everything," and suddenly I felt too tired. I seem the only manager in this firm who is allowed – indeed expected – to complain about practical everyday details. When I start doing it our directors exchange little smiles, stop listening and retreat into private dreamlands. They think everyday practical details are not their business but the business of Mulgrew the buildings manager and Tramworth the accountant. Nobody, not even Mulgrew, denies that what I ask to be done ought to be done, but only he and Tramworth can authorize it so it is never done. I have raised items on this list at meetings from last month to years ago. You joined us less than two months ago so the first and longest item on the list may strike you as an accident. I assure you that something of the sort happens every winter.

1.   Heat. Monday was bloody cold. I asked Mulgrew to do something about this. He agreed to turn up the thermostat a little but not much because

part of upstairs was already warm – the part where he and Tramworth have their office. Soon after 10 a.m. I noticed it was cold. When this happens I know others are freezing, so tried to find Mulgrew with the usual results. He had gone to the Sauchiehall Street depot, but when I phoned there he had just left it and nobody knew where he was supposed to be. By this time people on my floor were asking me to do something about the cold and I actually met people from upstairs who were touring the building in search of heat. I phoned Mulgrew's office again and got Tramworth. He suggested I tell people to work harder or jump up and down in order to stay warm. I refrained from telling him this should be his job as it was his staff who were touring the building and on whose behalf I was trying to contact Mulgrew. I suppose people ask help from me instead of their own managers because I do not treat everyone with complaints as if they are troublemakers. Mulgrew appeared around lunch time. Either Tramworth did not tell him the problem or he ignored it. I caught him before he left the building a second time. He did go to the thermostat then and discovered it had been turned down from 30 to 16 degrees before he turned it up. Since only he can have turned it down how he made this mistake escapes me. During the afternoon the place slowly warmed. People were and are annoyed about this because:

(a) The discomfort stops them working properly,

making them feel useless as well as frozen.
(b) Heating is decided by people who are outside the building, or cocooned in an office when in it.
(c) This has been going on for years.

2. The route to the emergency exit is as badly blocked as ever. Mulgrew is our fire safety officer as well as buildings manager, so draws an extra salary to stop that kind of thing happening. He can stop it by ordering new storage racks. I wish he was less friendly with the local fire precautions inspector. Mulgrew always knows when a thorough inspection will happen so the inspector never sees the usual state of the place. Sometimes, (like today), the inspector calls in without warning, but in that case (like today) he never looks at the emergency exit. God help us if we have a fire when a *thorough* inspection has not been scheduled.

3. The top tread of the stairs is still as loose as when Mrs Macleod tripped and fell down them. You may remember the doctor said she was lucky not to have broken her back. Senior management seem to think a handwritten warning notice has solved the problem for the foreseeable future, but one day we might have a short-sighted visitor. The other treads also need attention.

4. Nothing has been done about the window behind Helen Scrimgeour's desk. Its dangerous

state was first reported a year ago.

5. Handrail on the spiral staircase is loose.

6. Radiators in the ladies' loo are not turned on.

7. Heatscreens. (Outstanding for two years.)

8. A light in the loading bay. (Outstanding for more than two years.)

Of course you know the reasons for the above. The directors' offices are in the George Square depot, so they are glad to spend as little as possible on maintaining and keeping comfortable a building never noticed by the general public. Yet most of the firm's employees work in this dirty old building, which houses the most profitable part of their business. Can Phimister and Henry Pitt not see that every hundred pounds saved on heating means that a hundred people do two thirds of the work they would normally do?

I realize this letter is not fair to you, Lumley. The directors and senior management have put you here to protect them from this kind of information. It embarrasses them to hear about staff problems from the mouths of the staff, they do not want to know about our problems at all. We are learning to handle the new computer which, properly used, should make us more efficient.

While learning we must go on handling orders and dispatches in the old way, which makes us even less efficient. Since the directors and senior management know nothing about computers they thought everything would at once improve, not get worse, as soon as they bought one, so now they are trying to avoid paying for anything else. But why does Henry Pitt insist on handling all incoming mail and send every tiny complaint straight to my staff after marking it *top priority – attend to this at once*? They spend hours making sure that a garage in Stromness or Brighton gets a single free replacement while factories in the Midlands are kept waiting, though they have ordered 500 and paid for them in advance. Henry Pitt's grandfather founded this firm, he is a major shareholder and has been with it all his life, but his only management experience is with our depots. He should send all orders and complaints straight to me and Mrs Mcleod, who've been working here for fifteen years so know the priorities. The staff here sometimes feel that the directors and senior management are conspiring to STOP us doing the work they employ us to do. The idea is insane but that is what we sometimes feel, though they have probably just lost interest in us.

Or is it an insane idea? Henry Pitt is over sixty, must soon retire and has no children. Phimister has his Loch Lomond fish farm. It began as a rich man's hobby because he enjoys messing

about in boats, but Mulgrew and Tramworth gave
him a lot of help and a recent article in *The Scots Magazine* said it was now profitable. It also quoted him as saying, "I want a cleaner, fresher life for my children. Modern cities are becoming intolerable." If Pitt and Phimister sold the business they would make quite a lot. Since it is the only remaining firm of its kind in Scotland the buyers would almost certainly be southerners who would keep the depots but shut this distribution centre. Do you think we are coming to that, Lumley? It has happened with ship building, the car industry, textiles, steel, sanitary engineering et cetera.

I have had another idea. If they decide to sell us off could not a few of us (me, you, Mrs Macleod, Helen Scrimgeour, Colin Shand and maybe some others) put in an offer for the distribution part – this part – and buy it and run it for ourselves? We know how to do it. I would really like to talk to you about this. You are the only member of the senior management who listens to what I say and knows what I mean. Also, if a sell-out is being planned you will be one of the first to know about it. You also went to the same school as Phimister, so understand these things much better than I do.

HOUGH I SPEAK with the tongues of men and of angels, and have not Love, I am become as sounding brass, or a tinkling cymbal. And though I have the gift of prophecy, and understand all mysteries, and all knowledge; and though I have all faith, so that I could remove mountains, and have not Love, I am nothing. And though I bestow all my goods to feed the poor, and though I give my body to be burned, and have not Love, it profiteth me nothing.' – Paul wrote this in his first letter to the Christians of . . .

"Excuse me but I want to ask you one question, just one question. Are you a lesbian?"

"I am not a lesbian."

"That answer, if you will pardon me for saying so, is not satisfactory. For the last two Sundays I have watched you stroll in here at five-thirty, wearing jeans. You order a pint of lager, bring it to this corner and sit reading a book and shrugging off every man who tries to start a conversation with you. Why act that way if you arenae a lesbian?"

"That is your second question. You said you would ask just one."

"Aye, all right. I take your point. Fair enough." *Paul wrote this in his first letter to the Christians of Corinth, less than twenty years after Christ was crucified. And now, a question.*

What do we need most in life? What, if we suddenly lost it, would make us both feel, and be, worthless? Some Christians will answer: their religion. They think their lives are given meaning by their faith in God who made and sustains the universe and became Jesus of Nazareth. Well, they are wrong. Faith in God can make us very strong — for centuries it has enabled Christians to suffer and inflict, prolong and endure hideous agonies for the most splendid reasons. But it is not what God wants. Paul tells us why: 'Though I have all faith, so that I could remove mountains, and have not Love, I am nothing.' 'Though I give my body to be burned, and have not Love, it profiteth me nothing.'

*In many (not all) Bibles you will read
'charity' where I have written 'Love'. Paul used
a Greek word meaning 'loving respect'—the
deepest affection possible between people.
Charity used to mean that in English, but has
come to mean 'goodness to people who are badly
off.' This sort of goodness can be a wonderful
expression of Love, but is not Love itself. People
have founded hospitals . . .*

"Excuse me, I know I'm butting in again but I have
something to say which will do you good if you
will only listen to me and not lose your temper.
There is only one reason why a man or a woman
comes to a pub and it is not the booze. You could
easily be drinking cans of lager in the privacy of
your ain hame and it would be cheaper, for
Christ's sake. So like everybody who comes to a
pub you are here for the company, so why shut me
out by sticking your nose in a book? I mean no
offence, but you are a very attractive woman, in
spite of wearing jeans and no being very young. I
cannae be too plebeian nor too old for ye neither.
You would have gone to a pub higher up Byres
Road if you wanted posher or younger company."
"I will tell why I come here if you promise to leave
me in peace afterward."
"Fair enough. Fire away."
"I have two daughters and a son in their late teens,
and a homeloving husband who works in the
finance department of the district council. They
leave all housework to me but I enjoy keeping the

house clean and tidy so can honestly say I do not
feel exploited. I do voluntary work for Save the
Children, and Amnesty International. I have no
money worries, family worries, health worries and
used to think I was one of the luckiest people alive.
Nothing seems to have changed but my life is now
almost unbearable. No doubt a doctor would
blame the menopause and prescribe Valium. I
think I've suddenly started seeing myself clearly
after eighteen years of looking after other people.

"You see my father was a Church of Scotland
minister and I loved him a lot – he was kind and
distant and mysterious. Like most Protestant
clergymen he was probably embarrassed by
drawing wages to go about looking better than
other people. The best clergymen get over their
embarrassment by working hard – running soup
kitchens, getting decent clothes for families who
can't afford them, visiting the lonely. My father's
church was in a posh suburb. Everybody in the
congregation seemed prosperous so we never
noticed the poor. He spent most of the time
between meals in his study, writing sermons for
Sunday. They were no better than other ministers'
sermons but his elocution and manners were
perfect, old ladies loved him, everybody admired
what they called his *unworldliness*. I only noticed
he was a fraud when I got to university.

"I enjoyed university because I believed I was

becoming better – better than him. I took Divinity and was preparing for the ministry . . .

" Wait a minute! You were studying to be a Church of Scotland minister?"

"Yes."

"Since when has the Church of Scotland allowed women ministers?"

"Since the sixties. A woman applied for ordination and there was no law against it."

"Though not a churchgoer or a strict Christian I have strong Protestant sympathies, and women ministers just don't seem right."

"Then leave me alone."

"No no! I'm sorry! I mean go on and tell me what is wrong with your marriage. My own marriage is not what it should be. I will regard it as a great favour if you ignore my interruption and spill the beans."

"All right. At university I joined a lot of societies – The Students' Christian Union, The Iona Community and Christians Against the Bomb. I had lots of friends who knew the world should and could be improved, and worked at it. But I began to feel something essential was missing from our lives – God. When I prayed I never felt closer to anyone. When I asked my religious friends how it felt to have God beside them they got embarrassed and changed the subject. Why are you grinning?"

"I know a bloke who feels God is with him all the time. The two of them go along Dumbarton Road together having frantic arguments, though we only hear what poor Jimmy says. 'I refuse to do it!' he shouts. 'You have no right to order me to do it! You'll get me the jail!' It seems God keeps telling him to smash the windows of Catholic bookshops."

"Yes, anybody who hears the voice of God nowadays is deluded. God said everything we need to know through the words of Jesus. But many sane people have felt God's presence since Jesus died. I used to read their autobiographies, they made me envious – and angry too. Some were saintly junkies, hooked on the Holy Ghost like cocaine addicts to their dealer, passing miserable weeks waiting for the next visitation. I was not so greedy. One wee visit would have satisfied me – I could have lived on the memory ever after. But if I became a minister of God without once feeling God loved and wanted me I knew I would end up a fraud like my father. The nearest I could get to God was in books, which were not enough. I lost interest in Christianity, fell in love with a healthy agnostic and married instead. It was easy."

"Do you know what I'm going to tell you?"

"Yes – that it was the best thing which could have happened to me. If you shut your mouth and listen as you promised I'll explain why it was not.

"I've always found it easy to give the people nearest me what they want. As a student I worked perfectly with busy, excitable, eccentric Christian Socialists. After marriage I perfectly suited someone who wanted a wife to give him polite well-dressed children and a home where he could entertain his friends and colleagues and their wives. So marriage completely changed my character and maybe destroyed part of it. Nowadays I want to hear people talk about the soul, and God, and how to build bridges between them. I can meet these people in books – nowhere else – but my friends and children and husband give me no peace to read. They can't stop telling me news and discussing problems which strike me as increasingly trivial. I can't help listening and smiling and answering with an automatic sympathy I no longer feel. They cannot believe my reading matters. If I locked myself for an hour in the bedroom with a book and a can of lager they would keep knocking on the door and asking what was wrong. Now you know why I come here to read."

Some have founded hospitals for the poor because they wanted popularity or fame or felt guilty about their wealth. That is why Paul says 'Though I bestow all my goods to feed ...'
"Wait a minute. Have you tried going to church?"
"Often. It was what I usually did on Sundays but the prayers now sound meaningless to me, the hymns like bad community singing, the sermons as dull as my father's. Two weeks ago, without telling my family, I came here instead. Nobody I know will ever come to this pub, and it doesn't

play loud music. And I like the company, you were right about that."

"Eh?"

"Yes. I feel less lonely among people who are quietly talking and drinking – as long as they don't talk to me or lay their hand on my thigh."

"It won't happen again."

"Enjoying a pint and a read here is my Sunday service. Can I go on with it?"

"Aye. Sure. Of course. I meant no offence."

That is why Paul says, 'Though I bestow all my goods to feed the poor, and have not Love, it profiteth me nothing.' Peter says the same: 'Above all things have fervent love among yourselves.' John goes further: 'God is love.' And Jesus gave us a commandment which makes all laws needless for those who obey it: 'Love the Lord your God with all your heart and all your mind and all your soul, and your neighbour as yourself.' Remembering this, let us return to Paul.

Love suffereth long, and is kind; Love envieth not, and is not puffed up, doth not behave itself unseemly, seeketh not her own, is not easily provoked . . .

"Excuse me for butting in again but I've been giving some thought to your problem."

is not easily provoked . . .

"I think I see where the solution lies."

is not easily provoked . . .

"I know as well as you do that sex is not the reason for everything but . . ."

"YAAAAEEEE HELP BARMAN HELP!!!!"

"For Christ's sake . . ."

"Right, what's happening here?"

"Barman, this man nipped me."

"She's a liar, I never touched her!"

"Yes you touched me. I asked you again and again not to, but for twenty minutes you've sat here nip nip nipping my head like, like a bloody husband. Please get him off me, barman."

"Right you – outside. This is not the first time I've seen you at this game. Out you go."

"Don't worry, I'm leaving. But let me tell you something: that woman is a nut case – a religious nut case."

"Shut your mouth and clear out."

is not easily provoked, thinketh no evil; rejoiceth not in iniquity, but rejoiceth in the truth; beareth all things, believeth all things, hopeth all things, endureth all things. Love never faileth; but whether there be prophecies, they shall fail; whether there be tongues, they shall cease; whether there be knowledge, it shall vanish away.

"The old man who was pestering you has gone, Missus. You won't even see him in the street outside – he's slipped into the pub next door."

"Thank you. I'm sorry I troubled you but he insisted on pestering me."

"I understand that Missus, and I'm very sorry that now I must ask you to leave also."

"Why? *Why?*"

"Solitary women are liable to stir up trouble as you have just noticed. This is not your sort of pub. Try one nearer the top of the road."

"Will you allow me to finish my drink?"

"Certainly. Of course. Don't rush it, take your time. It's the last you'll be served here."

For we know in part, and we prophesy in part. But when that which is perfect is come, then that which is in part shall be done away. When I was a child, I spake as a child, I understood as a child, I thought as a child: but when I became a man I put away childish things. For now we see through a glass, darkly; but then face to face: now I know in part; but then shall I know even as also I am known. And now abideth faith, hope, Love, these three; but the greatest of these is Love.

"I'm sorry Missus but you have to leave now, at once, whether you've finished your pint or not. We cannot have a woman weeping in the corner of the bar. It spoils people's pleasure."

THE MARRIAGE FEAST

I MET JESUS CHRIST only once, in Cana, at some sort of marriage feast. I say "feast" because that word was distinctly printed on the invitation card, though it aroused expectations which were not fulfilled, for the parents of the bride had either pretentions beyond their incomes or were downright stingy. The waiters' tardiness in refilling our glasses suggested the booze was in short supply, and long before we finished the unappetizing main course there was none to be had. The person most obviously upset about this was a little old Jewish lady who had already (I seem to remember) consumed more than her fair share of the available alcohol.

"They have no wine!" she hissed in a stage whisper which was heard throughout the room and embarrassed everyone except (apparently) our hosts. I was compelled to admire their equanimity in the face of so audible a hint. The little lady was addressing a man who looked like – and actually was – both her son and a carpenter wearing his best suit. Like many mothers she was blaming her offspring for other people's faults, but his reaction surprised me.

"Woman!" he declared, "My time is not yet come!"

This struck us all as a meaningless remark, though I later realized it was advance publicity for his brief, disastrous career as a faith healer. However, a moment afterwards he beckoned the head of the catering staff, and whispered something which resulted in more wine being served.

At the time I assumed Christ had himself paid for extra booze so was almost inclined to feel grateful, but Freddie Tattersal (who is also Jewish) told me, "Remember that Christ belonged to the self-employed tradesman class, and that sort don't lash out money in acts of reckless generosity. There must still have been a lot of wine at that feast, but the waiters were saving it for themselves and the guests at the main table. Christ put the fear of God into the caterers by threatening to make a stink if they did not serve everyone equally, especially him – and he would have done it! They probably watered the plonk to make it go round." I still find this hard to believe. The plonk they served later was nothing to boast of but it was genuine plonk. I now believe I met Christ in one of his better moods. He was an unpleasant person who went about persuading very ordinary fishmongers and petty civil servants to abandon their jobs and wives and children and go about imitating him! There were a great many such self-appointed gurus in the sixties. Who cares about them nowadays?

BECAUSE OF A mistake (though I do not know whose) someone was shut in a windowless room with nothing to look at but a door which could only be opened from outside, a lavatory pan and a wall poster showing the face of the nation's ruler. After imagining a great many dealings with this official the prisoner tried to find pleasure in a landscape behind the face. This first soothed by its suggestion of spaciousness, then annoyed by its completely tame nature. On one side well-cultivated farms receded to a distant line of blue hills, on the other was a seat of government, a cathedral, university, and very clean factory and workers' residential block. There were no clumps

of forest or winding rivers to explore; the bland
distant hills clearly contained no ravines, torrents, cliffs, caverns or mountain passes, they were a mere frontier, shutting off the horizon. Though designed to advertise a sunnier world than the electrically lit cell, the poster showed the inside of a larger jail.

On the brink of melancholy madness the prisoner found a pencil on the floor behind the lavatory pan. When this had been carefully nibbled to a sharp point it might have been used to draw anything on the whitewashed walls: faces of friends, bodies of lovers, the scenery of great adventures. Not able to draw these convincingly the prisoner carefully drew a full-size copy of the room's unopenable door, with one difference. The drawn door had a key in the lock, and it could be turned. Then the prisoner turned the lock, opened the door and walked out. Though describing how fantasy works this is a realistic story. Free will being the essence of mind, everyone who feels trapped must imagine escapes, and some of them work. New arts and sciences, new religions and nations are created this way. But the story of the door can be told with a less happy ending.

A blind man living alone in a municipal housing scheme heard people breaking through his front door, so phoned the local police station. While he was asking for help the housebreakers got to him and knocked him down. They were policemen who had mistaken his door for the door of someone they suspected of selling dangerous drugs without a licence. The mistake was discovered when one of the housebreakers lifted the telephone receiver and found he was talking to a colleague. He told the colleague in the police station not to worry, because the blind householder would be *stitched up*. So the blind man was summoned to a court of law and charged with assaulting the police while they were trying to do their duty.

In Britain all emergency phonecalls to police stations are recorded twice: once by the police stations for the use of the police: once by the British telecommunication company for the use of the caller. The blind man's defence lawyer played the Telecom recording to prove that his client was innocent, pointing out that *stitched up* was slang for arrested on false evidence. The police witness agreed that stitched up meant that in criminal slang, but explained that in police slang it meant *properly arrested with no hint of falsehood or perjury in the procedure*. The sheriff on the bench (magistrates are called sheriffs in Scotland) believed the police witness, since our nation will sink into anarchy if magistrates distrust the police. But the blind man was neither fined nor imprisoned, as might easily have happened in an old-fashioned fascist or communist nation.

Like the sheriff on the bench my sympathy is
mainly with the police. Opening a door with *the big key* (which is police slang for sledgehammer) is a desperate deed, even if you think someone behind the door is wicked, and that if you grab them fast enough you may find proof of this. Nearly all our experience and education, besides the natural law of do-as-you-would-be-done-by, teaches us to handle doors gently. They are usually quiet, unthreatening, protective creatures. Some of our dearest joys and most regular functions have been made easier by them, so smashing one MUST feel like punching a face, or bombing pedestrians from an aeroplane in broad daylight. We may earn a wage by doing it, we may believe we are defending decency and justice by it, but we cannot help feeling abnormally excited, so mistakes are inevitable. I also sympathize slightly with the blind man, for I am not one of those who think everyone in a municipal housing scheme deserves what is done to them. The man's blindness may not have been his own fault, and may have stopped him seeing he ought to live in a better part of the city. But he should certainly have used his imagination, which would have let him see in the dark.

The big key unlocked the blind man's door in 1990 when Glasgow was the official Culture Capital of Europe. The story was not reported by the press. I give it here because the police, like the prisoner in my first story, found themselves in a terrible situation but imagined a way out. They created a fictional exit which worked.

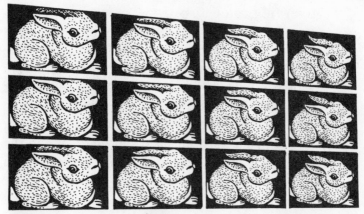

ILLIONS of people lived in rooms joined by long windowless corridors. The work which kept their world going (or seemed to, because they were taught that it did, and nobody can ever be taught the exact truth) their work was done on machines in the rooms where they lived, and the machines rewarded them by telling them how much they earned. Big earners could borrow money which got them better rooms. The machines, the money-lending and most of the rooms belonged to three or four organizations. There was also a government and a method of choosing it which allowed everyone, every five years, to press a button marked STAY or

CHANGE. This kept or altered the faces of the politicians. The politicians paid themselves for governing, and also drew incomes from the organizations which owned everything, but governing and owning were regarded as separate activities, so the personal links between them were dismissed as coincidences or accepted as inevitable. Yet many folk – even big earners in comfortable rooms – felt enclosed without knowing exactly what enclosed them. When the government announced that it now governed a wholly new world many people were greatly excited, because their history associated new worlds with freedom and wide spaces.

I imagine a man, not young or especially talented, but intelligent and hopeful, who pays for the privilege of emigrating to the new world. This costs nearly all he has, but on the new world he can win back four times as much in a few years if he works extra hard. He goes to a room full of people like himself. Eventually a door slides open and they filter down a passage to the interior of their transport. It resembles a small cinema. The émigrés sit watching a screen on which appears deep blackness spotted with little lights, the universe they are told they are travelling through. One of the lights grows so big that it is recognizable as a blue and white cloud-swept globe whose surface is mainly sun-reflecting ocean, then all lights are extinguished and, without

alarm, our man falls asleep. He has been told that
a spell of unconsciousness will ease his arrival in the new world.

He wakens on his feet, facing a clerk across a counter. The clerk hands him a numbered disc, points to a corridor, and tells him to walk down it and wait outside a door with the same number. These instructions are easy to follow. Our man is so stupefied by his recent sleep that he walks a long way before remembering he is supposed to be in a new world. It may be a different world, for the corridor is narrower than the corridors he is used to, and coloured matt brown instead of shiny green, but it has the same lack of windows. The only new thing he notices is a strong smell of fresh paint.

He walks very far before finding the door. A man of his own sort sits on a bench in front of it staring morosely at the floor between his shoes. He does not look up when our man sits beside him. A long time passes. Our man grows impatient. The corridor is so narrow that his knees are not much more than a foot from the door he faces. There is nothing to look at but brown paintwork. At length he murmurs sarcastically, "So this is our new world."
His neighbour glances at him briefly with quick little shake of the head. An equally long time passes before our man says, almost explosively,

"They promised me more room! Where is it? Where is it?"

The door opens, an empty metal trolley is pushed obliquely through and smashes hard into our man's legs. With a scream he staggers to his feet and hobbles backward away from the trolley, which is pushed by someone in a khaki dust-coat who is so big that his shoulders brush the walls on each side and also the ceiling: the low ceiling makes the trolley-pusher bend his head so far forward that our man, retreating sideways now and stammering words of pain and entreaty, stares up not at a face but at a bloated bald scalp. He cannot see if his pursuer is brutally herding him or merely pushing a trolley. In sheer panic our man is about to yell for help when a voice says, "What's happening here? Leave the man alone Henry!" and his hand is seized in a comforting grip. The pain in his legs vanishes at once, or is forgotten.

His hand is held by another man of his own type, but a sympathetic and competent one who is leading him away from the trolley-man. Our man, not yet recovered from a brutal assault of a kind he has only experienced in childhood, is childishly grateful for the pressure of the friendly hand. "I'm sure you were doing nothing wrong," says the stranger pleasantly, "You were probably just complaining. Henry gets cross when he hears one of our sort complain. Class prejudice is the root of it. What were you complaining about? Lack of space, perhaps?"

Our man looks into the friendly, guileless face beside him and, after a moment, nods: which may be the worst mistake of his life, but for a while he does not notice this. The comforting handclasp, the increasing distance from Henry who falls farther behind with each brisk step they take, is accompanied by a feeling that the corridors are becoming spacious, the walls farther apart, the ceiling higher. His companion also seems larger and for a while this too is a comfort, a return to a time when he could be protected from bullies by bigger people who liked him. But he is shrinking, and the smaller he gets the more desperately he clutches the hand which is reducing his human stature. At last, when his arm is dragged so straight above his head that in another moment it will swing him clear of the floor, his companion releases him, smiles down at him, wags a kindly forefinger and says, "Now you have all the space you need. But remember, God is trapped in you! He will not let you rest until you amount to more than this."

The stranger goes through a door, closing it carefully after him. Our man stares up at a knob which is now and forever out of his reach.

THE TRENDELENBURG POSITION

OME IN, come in, Mrs Chigwell. Sit down. My partner is sorry he cannot attend to you, as arranged, but there will be no complications. His wife was unexpectedly struck down by something this morning and though (thank goodness) she is not exactly at death's door he would find it hard to concentrate on your (thank goodness) smaller problem. His mind might wander, his hand tremble, so you are safer with me. His X-rays indicate two fillings, one of them a wee toaty tiddler of a job, and I am so sure of my skill that I promise you will feel no pain if I work without anaesthetic. But maybe you are nervous and want it, even so? No? Splendid. I am starting

the motor – which lowers and tilts the chair – so easily and smoothly that your heart and semi-circular canals have suffered no shock or disturbance. The Trendelenburg Position – that is what we call the position you are in, Mrs Chigwell. This chair gets you into it, and out of it, in a manner which ensures you cannot possibly faint. I wonder who Trendelenburg is.

Or was. Rinse your mouth. Let me – keek – inside. Oho! And if you want to sneeze, gargle, hiccup or blow your nose just raise a finger of your left hand and I will stop what I am doing almost at once but here goes. Chigwell. Chigwell. An English name. Yes there are a lot of your kind in Scotland nowadays, but you'll never hear me complain. Do I bother you, talking away like this? No? Good. You probably realize I do it to stop your imagination wandering, as it would tend to do if I worked in perfect silence. There is, let us face it, something inherently sinister in lying absolutely passive while a stranger in a white coat – no matter how highly qualified – does things you cannot see to this hole in your head – between your jaw and your brain; inside this wee toaty cavity – I am opening – in a bone of your skull. Even the presence of Miss Mackenzie, my assistant here, might not stop your subconscious mind cooking up weird fantasies if we dentists, like barbers, had not a professional tendency to gossip. Which reminds me of a cartoon I saw in a bound volume of old Punch magazines : a barber says, "How would you like your hair cut sir?" to a bored-looking aristocratic type slumped in his chair who says, "In a silence broken only by the busy snipsnap of the scissors." Sometimes I hear myself saying ridiculous things, utterly absurd things, just to avoid that deathly silence, but if you prefer silence just raise two fingers of your right hand and silent I will be. But you like the chatter? Good, rinse your mouth again.

No, my worst enemy could never accuse me of being a Scottish Nationalist. I don't approve of Scotland or Ireland – both Irelands – or England, Argentina, Pakistan, Bosnia et cetera. In my opinion nations, like religions and political institutions, have been rendered obsolete by modern technology. As Margaret Thatcher once so wisely said, "There is no such thing as society," and what is a nation but a great big example of our non-existent society? Margaret had the right idea – DENATIONALIZE! PRIVATIZE! When all our national institutions are privatized the British Isles will no longer be a political entity, and good riddance say I. The USSR has vanished. I hope the USA and the UK follow its example. Last week (a little wider please) a man said to me, "If you refuse to call yourself a Scot – or a Briton – or a Tory – or a Socialist – or a Christian what DO you call yourself? What do you believe in?"

"I am a Partick Thistle supporter," I told him, "and

I believe in Virtual Reality."

Do you know about Partick Thistle? It is a non-sectarian Glasgow football club. Rangers FC is overwhelmingly managed and supported by Protestant zealots, Celtic FC by Catholics, but the Partick Thistle supporters anthem goes like this:

> *We hate Roman Catholics,*
> *We hate Protestants too,*
> *We hate Jews and Muslims,*
> *Partick Thistle we love you . . .*

My friend Miss Mackenzie is looking distinctly disapproving. I suspect that Miss Mackenzie dislikes my singing voice. Or maybe she's religious. Are you religious Miss Mackenzie? No answer. She's religious.

Fine. Rinse your mouth. Second filling coming up and I insist on giving you a wee jag, but you won't feel it. Did you feel it? Of course not.

My wife disagrees with me. She's a Scottish Nationalist and a Socialist. Can you imagine a more ridiculous combination? She's a worrier, that woman. She's worried about over-population, industrial pollution, nuclear waste, rising unemployment, homelessness, drug abuse, crime, the sea level, the hole in the ozone layer.

"Only a democratic government responsive to the will of the majority can tackle these problems," she says.

"How will it do that?" say I.

"By seizing the big companies who are polluting and impoverishing and unemploying us," says she, "and using the profits on public work, education and health care."

"You'll never get that," I tell her, "because prosperous people don't want it and poor people can't imagine it. Only a few in-betweeners like you believe in such nonsense." (You have probably guessed she is a school teacher.) "By the year 2000," I tell her, "these problems will have been solved by the right kind of head gear. Even a modern hat of the broad-brimmed sort worn by Australians and Texans and Mexicans will protect you from skin cancer. Hatters should advertise them on television. TO HELL WITH THE OZONE LAYER — WEAR A HAT!"

Hats, Mrs Chigwell, hats. At the start of this century everybody wore them : toppers for upper-class and professional men, bowlers for the middling people, cloth caps for the workers. Bare headed folk were almost thought as shocking as nudists because their place in the social scale was not immediately obvious. I suspect that hats became unfashionable because we passed through a liberty, equality and fraternity phase – or imagined we were in one. But we're coming out of it again, and by the end of the century everybody will have head gear. Their sanity will depend on it. Am I boring you? Shall I change the subject? Would you like to suggest another topic of conversation? No? Rinse your mouth out all the same.

The hat of the future – in my opinion – will be a broad-brimmed safety helmet with hinged ear-flaps and a mouth-piece which can be folded down to work as a mobile telephone. It will also have a visor like old suits of armour or modern welders have, but when pulled down over your face the inside works as a telly screen. The energy needed to drive these sets could be tapped straight from the action of the viewer's heart – it would use up less energy than walking down a flight of stairs. The difference between one hat and another will be the number of channels you can afford. The wealthy will have no limit to them, but the homeless and unemployed will benefit too. I am not one of these heartless people who despise the unemployed for watching television all day. Without some entertainment they would turn to drugs, crime and suicide even more than they're doing already, but these video helmets will provide richer entertainment than we get nowadays from these old-fashioned box TVs which to my eyes already look prehistoric – relics of the wood and glass age – BVR – Before Virtual Reality. You've heard about virtual reality? Yes? No? It's a helmet of the sort I've just described. You wear it with a kind of overall suit equipped with electronic pressure pads so that you not only see and hear, but feel you're inside the television world you are watching. Miss Mackenzie is pulling faces at me because she knows what I am going to say and thinks it may shock you since it refers to sex. But I promise that not one bad word will pass my lips. These helmet suits not only give sensations of life and movement in beautiful exciting surroundings. They also, if you desire it, give the visual and sensual experience of an amorous encounter with the partner of your choice. Perhaps Clint Eastwood in your case, Mrs Chigwell. Silvana Mangano in mine, although it shows how old I am. Any professional person who remembers Silvana Mangano in *Bitter Rice* is obviously on the verge of retirement. Or senility. And so, I am afraid, is she. Not that I ever saw her in *Bitter Rice* – a film for Adults Only. I only encountered the first love of my life through her posters and publicity photos. I wonder what Silvana Mangano looks like nowadays?

Excuse me while I wash my hands. We are on the verge of completion. You're still quite comfortable? Good. Here we go again and remember I am talking nonsense, nothing but nonsense.

The hat of tomorrow – an audio-visual helmet with or without the suit – will not only release you into an exciting world of your own choice; it will shut out the dirty, unpleasant future my wife keeps worrying about. It will give marijuana or heavy drug sensations without damaging the health. Of course intelligent people like you and I, Mrs Chigwell, will use it for more than escapist entertainment. We will use it to talk to friends, and educate ourselves. Children of four will be fitted with helmets giving them the experience of a spacious, friendly classroom where beautiful, wise, playful adults teach them everything their parents want them to know. Schools will become things of the past and teachers too since a few hundred well scripted actors will be able to educate the entire planet. And think of the saving in transport! When the lesson stopped they could take the helmet off and bingo – they're home again. Unless the parents switch them onto a babysitter channel.

"All right!" says my wife after hearing me thus far, "What about homelessness? Your helmets can't shut out foul weather and poisoned air."

"They can if combined with the right overalls," I tell her. "In tropical countries, like India, homeless people live and sleep quite comfortably in the streets. Now, it is a widely known fact that our armed forces have warehouses stacked with suits and respirators designed to help them survive on planet Earth after the last great nuclear war has made everybody homeless. But the last great nuclear war has been indefinitely postponed. Why not add Virtual Reality visors and pressure pads to these suits and give them to our paupers? Tune them into a channel of a warm Samoan beach under the stars with the partner of their choice and they'll happily pass a rainy night in the rubble of a burnt-out housing scheme and please rinse your mouth out. Don't chew anything hard for another couple of hours. The chair – is now restoring you – to a less prone position.

Bye-bye, Mrs Chigwell. The receptionist will give you the bill, and it might be wise to arrange an appointment in – perhaps six months from now. Whatever the future of the human race it is not likely to dispense with dentists.

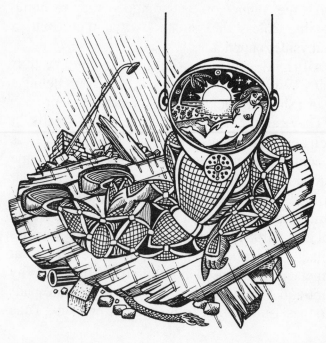

I DISCOVERED an odd thing about my left foot when about to pull on a sock this morning. In the groove between the second and third toe, reckoning from the big toe, is a small grey pellet of chewing-gum. I do not chew gum, or know or remember meeting anyone who does. I sometimes patter about this room in my dressing-gown and bare feet, but I never go out of it, and nobody comes here nowadays except the one who cares for me, who is Zoë I believe. And hope. Zoë would never play such a sly wee disturbing trick as putting a sticky sweet between the toes of a sleeping man. Her tricks were all bonny and lavish. I once came home to find that a friend had given her back money we had lent him, money we had stopped expecting to get back, though we needed it for food and rent. Zoë had spent half of it on food all right – we had food enough to last a fortnight. She had spent the rest on flowers. The bedroom floor was covered with vases, jugs, bowls, pans, basins, kettles so full of irises, lilacs and carnations that the bed seemed afloat in a small Loch Lomond of blue, purple and crimson petals. The scent nearly knocked me out. I had to be angry. I saw the loving goodness in that gesture, but had I encouraged lavishness we would have ended up homeless. She knew it, too. Once when I chose to be lavish she grew thoughtful, worried, then angry. She wanted me to be careful and mean so that she could be lavish, which does not explain how this chewing-gum arrived between my toes.

I do not believe in miracles. I believe the human mind can solve, rationally, any problem it recognizes and closely attends to. I decided not to finish dressing before I solved this one, though I usually earn my pocket-money and the right to stay here by working on the problem of time travel. I dropped the left sock on the floor (Zoë would pick it up) and from a sitting posture on the edge of the bed moved to a prone one on top of the quilt, which I must remember to call *a doovay*. If I do not learn to use the new words people keep inventing I will one day find I am talking a dead

language. I decided to tackle the problem of the
chewing-gum by a strategy combining Algebra, Euclidean Geometry and Baconian Induction; but feeling slightly cold in my semmit and single sock I first crept under the doovay and wrapped it round me because a snug body allows a clear mind.

GIVEN: M – Me who sometimes patter barefoot round this room. P – Pellet of gum stuck to the foot of M. UG – Unknown Gumchewer who is the source and prime mover of P. R – Room that M never leaves and UG never enters. W – World containing M, P, UG, R and other items and events.

REQUIRED: To find the likeliest event or events which could move P from the mouth of UG to the foot of M while preserving these conditions :–
1. M and UG remain ignorant of each other.
2. M is ignorant of P before finding P between his toes.
3. UG is ignorant of P's movement after it leaves him, but not while it leaves him. (Chewed gum only leaves a mouth by being swallowed or spat or removed by fingers and flicked into air or removed by fingers and attached to other item: all of which are conscious acts though soon forgotten.)

CONSTRUCTION! – Yes, I was now ready and able to set out the problem in geometrical space-time. I needed no pencil, paper, ruler or compasses. The decay of my organs and senses stops me doing or showing much to other people but strengthens my ability to see things inside. When completely dead to the world I expect to see it all perfectly. Without even closing my eyes I now visualize this:

The circles represent the world, the squares my room, the curved arrow the movement of the pellet into the room. Could I picture a single, simple event able to fire P for Pellet from the world outside onto the dark green mottled linoleum of this floor, from which the pressure and warmth of my foot later detached it? I pictured one easily.

Outside my window is an ash tree which looks insanely active, even when standing still. Three tall trunks diverge upward from the same root, and a few boughs or long branches fork from these in elegant curves, but most of them grow straight for a yard or more then, as if turning a corner, bend abruptly up or down or sideways, then undulate, zigzag, spiral, turn steep U-bends or suddenly explode outward into a lot of smaller branches, themselves as knotted and twisted as the tentacles of an arthritic squid. On the day I discovered the chewing-gum all these trunks, boughs, branches with their twigs and leaves were swaying, writhing, lashing about and reminding me they were rooted in a space of grass too smooth to be called a field, too rough to be called a lawn. I seemed to remember an asphalt path between the tree and window, but nearer the window than the tree. I easily imagined a stout sturdy man wearing boiler-suit, Wellington boots and cloth cap who strides along that path chewing a piece of gum which gets so flavourless that he fixes it to the ball of his thumb near the tip, bends his strong middle finger until the top edge of the nail touches the crease in the joint of his thumb then, using the thumb as a lock he builds up muscular pressure in the finger until, seeing an open window just ahead he mischievously aims his hand, unlocks his thumb and (without pausing in his stride) flicks slings catapults the pellet through onto the floor of the room, remaining as ignorant of me as I of him, at that moment. But the window is never open, so I must now seek a more complex though equally elegant solution to this problem.

Is? Now seek? This problem? I seem to be conducting my investigation in the present tense, though I certainly began it in the past. Time travel is unending. And I am sorry that the continually shut nature of the window has made that stout man improbable. For a moment I thought him a friend. I used to ask the one who cares for me (not Zoë, the other one) to open this window on sunny days, but he or she always said, "Sorry Dad no can do. It's against the rules. Why do you think we paid for air-conditioning?" I don't know why we paid for air-conditioning. I hate it. I learned to hate it in the 1980s when I was famous. I must have been, because people kept asking me how it felt to be famous. I always said, "Fine thank you, the perquisites are useful." The only perquisite I can now recall is flying from airport to airport all over North America, and sleeping in hotels, and appearing on platforms in conference centres. The airports, hotels and conference centres were very similar buildings with the same kind of furniture and windows which could not be opened because of the air conditioning. The air on the aeroplanes was fresher, though I could not open windows in those either. The only openable windows I saw in America belonged to cars speeding from one building to another, and would have poisoned me with exhaust fumes had I opened them. So I am used to breathing stale air, but it has damaged my memory. I do not know why people thought me famous, and asked me all over America, and why I went. It must have been a lie. When I was small, and passionately wanted to tell my mother something, and suddenly found I could not remember what it was, she always said, "It must have been a lie."

Wait a minute! I remember something said by a man who was introducing me to a big audience in Toronto or San Francisco or Quebec or Chicago or Montreal or Pittsburgh or Vancouver: *the most humane, far-sighted and lucid thinker the 20th century has known*, he called me. Yes yes. I travelled all over North America because I enjoyed the introductory speeches. This casts no light on the problem of the chewing-gum. I now know that UG could not flick or spit P for Pellet into this room. I am sure UG did not swallow it. Even if such a pellet could keep its colour, adhesiveness and integrity through a digestive tract, bowel gut and sphincter, its position after that would make its entry into my room improbable, whether UG defecated into a public sewage system or crapped behind a hedge. The following construction shows the likeliest chain of events. X represents a commonplace item in the world outside my room and later within it, having been brought from there to here by . . . but the item itself will indicate who brought it, so *visualize*!

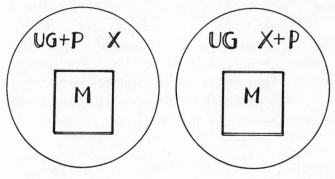

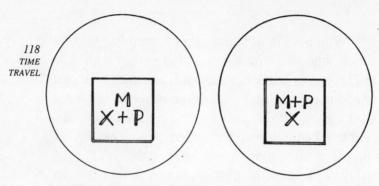

In this construction UG gets rid of P by casually sticking it onto X, which is carried into this room by Zoë, or by one of the other people who look after me, or by a visitor. But nobody has visited me for years so the fame did not last.

The problem had now been carried as near to a solution as this method allowed. I love the deductive method. No wonder its union of Greek geometry and Islamic algebra has seduced nearly every Continental thinker from Descartes to Levi-Strauss. However, to identify X I needed the inductive method, the practical British approach devised by the two Bacons and William of Occam. I was making a list of everything in the room I could have trodden on when my attention was distracted by the queer behaviour of a chair I had known for years. It stands between my bed and the window, but nearer the window than my bed. I must describe how it usually appears before telling how it acted on the day I found the pellet.

It is a low, light arm-chair with a wooden

frame, made not long after the Second World War
when money was more evenly spread, materials were in short supply, extravagant use of them was thought wasteful and ugly. Yet this chair does not look cheap. The elegantly tapered curves of the legs, the modestly widening, welcoming curve of the arms owe something to Japan and Scandinavia as well as aeroplane design. The seat and back are not thickly upholstered but so well supported that they feel perfectly comfortable. All the furniture Zoë owned looks and feels good. There was once another chair exactly like this one, and a sofa matching them. If people wanted a standard arm-chair I would honestly propose this one, as James Watt proposed a healthy workhorse without defects as the standard by which the power of artificial engines is measured to this day. Or does that last sentence show I am living in the past? Have engineers stopped measuring the strength of engines in horse-power? Are horses as extinct as whales? Is the Watt no longer a unit of electrical force? Watt was an 18th-century machinist from Greenock who invented the coal-fired water vapour engine. Has Rudolf Diesel's compression fired oil vapour engine supplanted Watt's terminology as well as his machines? Don't panic. I suspect this is a word problem, a quilt-doovay problem, not destruction-of-Scottish-achieve-ment-by-German-achievement problem. Unless I describe the usual colour of the chair the oddity of its conduct a week ago cannot be described.

The parts of the woodwork designed to be seen have been polished, stained and varnished to a medium chocolate colour that almost hides the grain. The upholstery is covered by a russet red fabric I found annoyingly bright before it faded. When in bed I view the chair in profile, like the chair Whistler's mother sits on, and see a tall narrow hole in the fabric of the back of the side, a hole through which at least twenty-four inches of pale unpolished unvarnished timber appear like a bone seen through an open wound. This hole has not been worn or torn open but shredded, as by a cat's claws – threads and shreds of fabric dangle down from the edges all round it. In the years when I rummaged in cupboards I found other evidence of a cat: a plastic feeding dish with FLUFFY printed on the sloping sides, and behind containers of Marmite Yeast Extract and Granny's Tomato Soup a tin of Whiskas Supermeat, Chicken and Rabbit Variety. Most sinister of all, behind the long-lost matching sofa I once saw a cardboard box more than two feet square with an arched hole like a door cut into one side, and crayoned over the sides and top a pattern suggesting brickwork, with the words CAT-PALACE, MOG-A-DEN and FLUFFY HOUSE. This writing was not in Zoë's hand. It suggested that before she helped me up from the pavement and brought me home here she loved another human being as well as a cat, somebody who enjoyed fishing. There was a wicker creel under the bed, an angling rod in the

wardrobe, waders in the lobby press. I said nothing
about these articles and one day I came home and they had gone. I said nothing, because out of sight is out of mind if I want it to be, nor did I mind Fluffy ripping at the chair. Cats invented themselves by clawing their way up and down tree trunks and scratching soil or grass over their excrement. Forbidding cats to scratch is like forbidding humans to cut their nails and hair. Also, the chair was not responding to Fluffy in the year I found the pellet. It was brightening and darkening. The dim russet fabric glowed and flickered, then leapt into dazzling vividness like when new, but with a moving pattern of leaves dancing over it in a very irregular way. This pattern (dull red on bright russet) was dove grey on creamy ivory over the exposed timber. For half a minute the chair persisted in this way then suddenly, like an exhausted dancer, slumped in two or three seconds back to its ordinary dull old colours. Had the chair been remembering leaves it had seen in earlier days?

Glancing through the window I noticed a remarkable coincidence. The leaves of the ash tree had the shapes and dancing movements of the pattern which had recently faded from the chair. And I saw another coincidence! Leaves, branches and trunks were flickering, lashing, swaying in the same direction and with the same turbulence as ragged whiteish-grey clouds in the sky beyond, clouds with shifting patches of blue and gleams of unpredictable sunlight between them. Without its underground roots every part of that tree would have flown off with the clouds, which shows the infectious force of a strong example. Had the air between the tree and clouds been visible I might have seen it rushing along too. For a moment I considered working out how the movements within the chair had been caused. People will pay a lot of money for objects that blaze and flicker, as television sets and games machines in public houses show. But I am too old to venture into show business. It is enough for me to passively enjoy the play of natural coincidences and actively enjoy the play of inward speculation. These two plays led to my famous discovery. Of course they did.

Einstein had died without establishing the unified field hypothesis, all the physicists had agreed the thing was impossible when I – a botanist – proved that every part and particle of the universe reflects every other part and particle and every past and eventual possibility inherent in each part and particle. My dissertation proving the identity of sense and motion in water lilies also proved the identity of sense and motion everywhere! And it cleared away all the paradoxes in Newtonian gravitation by showing that Kepler as well as Einstein had been right all along. Look at a star. Astronomers will say it is a distant sun or nebula, but even a moth can see it is a body of

light. We know it gives light because we live inside the radiance of the gift – live inside the star.
That twinkling little item is the core or central pip of a radiant fruit containing every other star and galaxy. My discovery angered many clever people, for by proving that loneliness is a convenient form of ignorance it left them nowhere to hide. "Nonsense!" roared the hearty pragmatists, "The light, heat, sounds et cetera given out by a body are not parts of the body, they are its excrement. Some bodies fling useful shit at us, some fling the dangerous kind so we need to identify the sources. The source you call a star is a mass of fissile material exuding beams essential to life and useful to navigators."

People with this self-centred view cannot be faulted. They want to be nothing but cockroaches in the larder of the universe, so have no interest in the rest of the palace. There was more dignity in the wrath of a great French scientist who was also a practising catholic, and so obsessed by the needless division between mind and body – so certain that only a God *outside* the universe could redeem what he thought was its horrible nature – that he would not see the regenerative side of my discovery.

"The silence of these vast spaces appals me," he said, talking about the gaps between the stars. I told him these gaps were spaces between the bodies in a busy market where light was being exchanged so rapidly our eyes could not catch it.

"Imbecile!" he cried, "Do you not know that whole blazing star systems are receding from us faster than light can travel, and will collapse into black cinders without a single ray or thought from them ever reaching the frozen cinder which was once our little world?"

I pointed out that while answering me his own mind had overtaken these blazing systems, had survived their extinction and returned to our own extinct world, enlivening it with one ray of impossible light, dignifying it with an impossibly gloomy thought. He frowned and said, "You are playing with words. Words are an expression of thought, not a physical force."

I pointed out that spoken sounds, though perhaps unable to open a closed mind, were as physical a force as dawn sunbeams that open the petals of daisies. But he so gloried in the faith he needed to face his appalling universe that he muttered, "Solipsist!" and turned his back on me. The Americans did not, or not at first. I expect they used me in propaganda for their space programme, or space race, or whatever the advertisers called it before the Russians made it pointless by stopping pretending to compete.

Having solved the universal problems I now need to exercise my brain with smaller matters like time travel, and where Zoë has been for the last two or three days, and Between Two Toes, or The Case of the Mysterious Pellet.

I cannot now say if I am solving the last of
these problems in the present or remembering how
I once solved it in the past but the time came (or
has come) when I made (or will make) a list of
items brought recently into my room from the
world outside: food, cleaned clothes and towels,
newspapers and letters. Then I made (or will
make) another list of items on the floor of the
room, items my foot could have pattered across:
the linoleum, a fringed rug and things often
dropped on these like food, clothes, towels,
newspapers and letters. Items common to both
lists should then be considered one at a time with
great care, for one of these must be item X. And I
have just remembered that letters and newspapers
should be on neither list. Nobody has written to
me for years, and I stopped taking papers during
the last great miners' strike in the 1980s when I
saw that Britain had again become a financial
oligarchy protected by the ancient fraud of a
two-party electoral system. But the lists are not
needed because I now see the gum MUST have
come from inside the sock I wore yesterday, a sock
which like all my clothes is washed in a machine
outside this room where the clothes of other
people (one of whom must be the Unknown
Gumchewer) are also washed. UG accidentally
attached the P for Pellet to a cardigan or other
woollen article. UG's helper (who is probably one
of mine too) put it in the drum of a machine whose
soapy solutions and hydraulic pressures dissolved

most of the dirt but only displaced P for Pellet from the cardigan to the toe of my sock while the sock was inside out: its invariable state after I pull it off at night. Zoë or whoever else looks after me turns the cleaned socks the right way round at night before setting out a cleaned pair for me to put on next day. The fact that all my socks are grey like the Pellet would prevent Zoë or the other one seeing and removing it. Eureka!

I basked in the elegance of this solution for two or three happy and peaceful minutes. Since discovering the Pellet I had been rolling it idly between the ball of my right-hand thumb and forefinger. I was about to flick it into a pail-shaped metal waste-bin near the bed when something in its soft, plastic adhesiveness made me doubt if it was chewing-gum at all. It was very like a more recent invention called Blu-Tack, first marketed in the 1970s (I think) as a means of attaching paper notices and light pictorial reproductions to surfaces without puncturing or staining the notices, reproductions and surfaces. But there are no such things in my room. I don't need them. Zoë's chair in front of the window, the ash tree outside it give me all the entertainment and food for thought I need. Or have I forgotten something? Look suspiciously, carefully, at all nearby surfaces. Yes, there is something I forgot.

Beside my bed is a small metal wardrobe with

wheels of a kind I have never before seen outside hospitals and homes for the chronically ill and disabled. On a side of this immediately opposite my face when I lie down is a paper document fastened by blobs of Blu-Tack at the two upper and the right-hand lower corner. This letter has a conventionally regal heading and a signature at the foot scribbled by Charles King number 3. The bit between signature and heading is very prettily printed or exquisitely typed, and congratulates me on attaining my hundredth birthday. Damn. Hell. F, no don't use fuck as a curse word. Remember what I wrote in that review of the 1928 edition of *Lady Chatterley's Lover* : "Lawrence has restored to tender uses what should be the tenderest word in any language." The *Glasgow Herald* sacked me for writing that review. I had guts in 1928. Perhaps that was my finest hour. But this letter which I tear down, crumple and fling into the waste-bin proves three unpleasant facts:

1. This is the 21st century.
2. Britain is still a damned and blasted monarchy.
3. I have not seen Zoë lately, or anybody else I know, because she and they died in the decade after Fluffy died, nearly twenty-five years ago.

I'm glad they left me Zoë's chair.
It makes time travel easier.

NEAR THE DRIVER

THIS intelligent, kind old lady was once a school-teacher, and it shows in her forthright manners and alert appearance. On the station announcement board she reads that the 11.15 Aquarian from Bundlon to Shaglow will leave from platform H, and this worries her. While aware that her memory is failing she is sure station platforms used to be numbered, not lettered, so why the change? And walking along the platform she sees the carriages have very small square windows with rounded corners. The last time she travelled by rail the windows seemed to be big long glass panels that stretched the entire side of each carriage with hardly any interruption. She also remembers when

carriages were divided into compartments like the
insides of stage coaches, each with a door in the middle of either side, a door whose window could be raised or lowered by fitting holes in a thick leather strap onto shining brass studs. The handles of these old doors were shining brass levers. She stops and examines a door of a carriage near the front of the modern train. It has neither window nor handle, just a square plastic button in the middle with PRESS engraved on it. She presses. The door slides up like a blind. She steps through and it snaps down behind her.

She finds herself peering along a central corridor with rows of three high-backed seats on each side, all facing her. The backs of the six front seats hide all but the rows in front. Beside one window a sturdy old man sits reading a newspaper published by the British Orthodox Communist Party. The teacher nods approvingly, for though never a Communist she approves of radical politics. Beside the old man is a housewife with a worried expression, beside the woman a restless little child wearing a blue canvas suit. The teacher, proud of her ability to read character at a glance, decides these are three generations of a family belonging to the skilled artisan class. Beside the opposite window a middle-aged, middle-class couple sit bolt upright staring straight ahead. They seem to be ignoring each other, but with another approving nod the teacher sees on the arm-rest between them the man's left hand clasping the woman's right. The teacher sits in the empty seat beside this couple, saying to nobody in particular, "I suppose modern trains look like aeroplanes because they travel nearly as fast! I regret that because I hate air travel, but I'm glad our compartment is close to the bit that pulls – the bit we called the engine in the days of steam. I feel safer when I'm near the driver."

"My father feels that way too, though he won't admit it. Will you Dad?" says the housewife, but the old man mutters, "Shut up Miriam."

"I feel that too dear," murmurs the rigid lady to her husband who murmurs, "I know you do dear. Please shut up."

The teacher at once thinks of the married couple as Mr and Mrs Dear. Delighted to have started a conversation before the journey begins she says, "In most railway accidents the train is struck in the rear, isn't it? So statistically speaking we are safer near the engine."

"That's stupid!" squeaks the child.

The mother says, "Don't be rude Patsy," but the teacher says eagerly, "Oh please, I'm a teacher! Retired! But I know how to handle difficult children. Why is what I said stupid Patsy?"

"Because in collisions the front of one train always hits the front or back of another, so the safest place in a train is always the middle."

The old man chuckles slightly, the other adults smile. After a moment of silence the teacher opens her purse, removes a coin and says, "Patsy, here is a bright new silver-looking fivepound coin. I give it to you because what I said was stupid and you were right to correct me."

The child grabs the coin. The other adults stare at the teacher and the conversation seems about to take a new direction when it is interrupted.

A melodious chime comes from the upholstery of the chair-backs then a quiet, firm, friendly voice saying, "Good day good people! This is Captain Rogers, your driver, welcoming you aboard the 1999 Aquarian from Bundlon to Shaglow, stopping at Bagchester, Shloo, Spittenfitney and Glaik. The Aquarian leaves at the end of this announcement, arriving at Bagchester exactly forty-one minutes later. Tea, coffee, sandwiches, will be served at half twenty-three hours, and in accordance with the latest stock-market reports, tea will be one point sixty pounds, coffee one point ninety-nine. Sandwiches are still last week's price and expected to remain stable for the duration of the journey. The bar is now open. British Rail trust you will have a comfortable trip. Thank you." Through the window on her left the teacher sees a pillar supporting the station canopy slide sideways, then a view of slate rooftops and shining tower blocks turning indistinct and vanishing.

The other passengers are complaining about

the price of tea. The teacher says, "But I'm glad they warned us. When is half twenty-three hours? It's a sign of senility for a retired teacher to admit this, but I can't grasp this new way of telling the time."

"Half past eleven, isn't it?" says the housewife uncertainly.

"A.m?"

"Yes, isn't it?"

The old man says abruptly, "Don't be daft Miriam. Half twenty-three hours is twelve from twenty-three and a half, which is eleven and a half, so half past eleven p.m."

"No no no!" cries the child excitedly, "Our headmaster says we shouldn't think about time in twelves because of computers and demicals. Computers can't count in demicals, so half twenty-three hours is half past twenty- three."

"Patsy!" says the old man in a low steady voice, "If you say one more word within the next ten minutes I shall remove the whole weight of my fist from the side of your jaw!" but the teacher merely sighs. Then says, "I wish they had let us keep the old noon with the twelve hours before and after it. But even the station clocks have changed. Instead of a circular face with all the hours and minutes marked around the edge, past AND future, we have a square panel with nothing in it but the minute we're at now. Nothing eight hours twenty minutes, then flick! – it's nothing eight hours twenty-one. That makes me feel trapped. Trapped, yet pushed at the same time. And I'm sure computers could be taught how to count in twelves, I hear some of them are quite intelligent. I hate that little flick when one minute becomes the next."

"I hate it too dear," murmurs Mrs Dear and, "So do I dear, please shut up," says her husband.

"Time and money!" says the teacher sighing again, "So much disappeared so suddenly: the little farthings with jenny wrens on them, thick brown threepennies, silver sixpences, the old ha'penny. Did you know, Patsy, that ha'pennies were once a whole inch in diameter, the size of the modern twopenny?"

"What's an inch?" says the child.

"Two point five three nine nine nine eight centimetres. And the old pennies were lovely huge lumps of copper, two hundred and forty to the pound, we shall not see their like again, with Britannia ruling the waves between a small battleship and the Eddystone lighthouse. Britannia was a real woman, you know. Not many people realize that. She was copied from a – a girl friend of the Merry Monarch, not Nell Gwynne. The old pennies had room for so much history on them. They were history! Even in the sixties you still found coins with young Queen Victoria's head on them, and the old Queen was so common we took her for granted. Just think! Every time we went shopping we were handling coins which had clinked in the pockets of Charles Dickens and

Doctor Pritchard the poisoner and Isambard Kingdom Brunel."

"It might interest you to know, madam," says Mr Dear, "That the weight of a modern penny, subtracted from a pre-decimal penny, left enough copper to construct circuits for nine hundred and seventy-three pocket television sets."

"But WAS IT?" shouts the old man so violently that everyone stares at him and Mr Dear says, "I beg your pardon?"

"The copper!" says the old man excitedly, "The copper saved by switching to a smaller currency was NOT used to make cheap television sets for the masses! It was used to build the circuits of an electronic nuclear defence system that cost the British tax-payer a hundred and eighty-three thousand MILLION pounds and was obsolete two years before it was finally installed!"

"I have no wish to discuss politics with you sir," says Mr Dear, looking out the window again. The old man snorts and concentrates on his paper.

The women are the most embarrassed by the ensuing silence. The mother sends Patsy to the buffet bar to buy a chocolate biscuit with her new coin, and in a low voice the teacher asks the mother the sex of her little child. The mother, also in a low voice, explains that she thinks there is too much sex nowadays, that her mother never mentioned it, that Patsy will make up her own mind as soon as he's old enough to choose. The

teacher nods approvingly, but says in her
experience children are grateful for a little guidance. The mother disagrees; says that all a child should learn from its parents is proper manners; says at least Patsy won't turn into one of these dreadful women's lib ladies – or a teddy boy. The old man surprises them by saying suddenly, "A cat."

"What's that Dad?" asks his daughter.

"Teddy boys were forties," he explains, "Beatniks fifties. Hippies sixties. Mods and rockers seventies. Punks eighties. And now they call themselves cool cats."

"Are you sure?" asks the teacher, "There have been so many strange names for young people – skinheads, bobby-soxers, flappers, knuts, mashers and macaronis – that I've started thinking of them as youths. The police reports always call them youths."

"And quite right too!" mutters Mr Dear, and would say more but again the musical warbling introduces the firm friendly voice.

"Good day good people – Captain Rogers here. We are making excellent time. On our left we are flashing past the reforested bings of the outer Bundlon slag depot, on our right are the soya fields of the British Golliwog Jam Corporation. I regret that a special stock-market news flash has obliged us to raise the price of coffee to two point forty pounds a cup –" (the passengers' cries of rage and disgust drown the announcement for a while) "– biscuits are expected to remain stable at least as far as Shloo. Passengers with an interest in transport will not need to be told that today is a special one for British Rail. In one and a half minutes it will be precisely the hundred and fiftieth anniversary of the exact moment when Isambard Kingdom Brunel –" ("Brunel!" gasps the teacher) "– tapped the last ceremonial rivet into the Grand Albert Royal Pennine Suspension Bridge: the first broad-gauge box-girder suspension bridge in the history of engineering. To honour the occasion we will now play you *The Railways of Old England*, orchestrated and sung by Sir Noël Coward. Through the length and breadth of Britain, in trains trundling through the lonely Pass of Killiecrankie or thundering across the Stockport viaduct, passengers are rising to their feet to hear Noël Coward sing *The Railways of Old England*."

There is a preliminary rolling of drums with a sombre yet challenging blast of trumpets. Mr Dear, Mrs Dear and the teacher rise to their feet and the mother seems about to do so when the old man hisses, "Miriam! Patsy! Stay exactly where you are."

"Excuse me sir," cries Mr Dear, "Are you not going to stand?"

"No I am NOT!"

"Oh please sh dear!" whispers Mrs Dear to her

husband who cries, "Shut up dear, I will not sh!
You sir, I gather are one of those left-wing militant
extremists who yearn for a discredited Bolshevik
railway system. Well the British railway system
has no harsher critic than myself. I was sorry when
they nationalized it, saddened when they axed off
the branch lines and appalled by how long the
government took to restore it to a responsible
private company. But despite its grisly past our
rail system was built by a combination of Irish
brawn, Scottish engineering and English financial
daring which made us once the foremost steam
railway empire in the universe. Does this mean
nothing to you?"

"Don't talk to me about British Rail!" yells the old
man over Noël Coward's brittle patriotic tenor, "I
worked all my life for British Rail. I was a fireman
from the old LMS days to when they brought in
bloody diesel! British Rail was destroyed by
people like you – bloody accountants and lawyers
and retired admirals on the board of directors –"

"That's ludicrous!" cries Mr Dear, and "Stop it
Dad!" cries the old man's daughter, but nothing
stops the flood of his articulate wrath: "– when
they nationalized us the government said 'British
Rail belongs to the people now' but who did we
get on the new board of directors? Linesmen?
Footplate men? Station-masters? Did we hell! We
got the same old gang – stockbrokers, lieutenant
colonels, civil servants with posh accents, the
gang that eventually sold us out to the car

manufacturers, the building societies and the oil corporations!"

"I am not listening to you!!" cries Mr Dear.

"I never thought you would," says the old man chuckling and picking up his paper again. The music has stopped. The others sit down, Mr Dear looking as if he would prefer to do something more violent. There is another embarrassing silence, then the teacher slips across the aisle to Patsy's seat and tells the old man quietly, "I was to a large extent entirely on your side in that little exchange, even though I stood up. I like the tune you see, and old habits die hard. But the title was inaccurate. Our railways are British, not English." She slips back to her seat as Patsy approaches shouting, "Mum Mum Mum!"

Patsy, terribly excited, is closely followed by a tall, lean, mildly amused looking man who says, "Good day good people! Does this small person belong to any of you?"

"Patsy," says the mother, "Where have you been?"

"Wandering far too near the engine for anyone's good," says the stranger.

"How very naughty of you, Patsy. Thank the nice man for bringing you back."

"But Mum!" says the child excitedly bumping its bottom up and down on the seat, "Nobody's driving this train! The driver's cabin's empty! I looked inside!"

Mrs Dear gives a little gasp of horror. The mother

says severely, "Patsy, that's not a very nice thing
to say, not with that bad rail accident in America last week. Apologize at once."

"But Mum, it really was empty!"

"Dear, I'm terribly worried," Mrs Dear tells her husband who says, "Don't be stupid dear, the kid's obviously gone the wrong way and blundered into the guard's van."

The teacher points out that the stranger said he found Patsy near the engine, but "The child knows nothing about mechanics!" declares Mr Dear, "Hardly anyone knows anything about mechanics nowadays. It wouldn't surprise me to learn that modern trains are driven from an obscure cabin somewhere in the middle."

"And it wouldn't surprise me!" cries the old man violently, "To learn that British Rail has sacked all its drivers and never told the public a word about it!"

The women gasp in horror, Mr Dear snorts, the stranger laughs and tries to speak, but the old man talks him down: "You needed a driver in the days of steam – two of them counting the fireman – tough men! Strong men who knew the engine and could clean it themselves, and grasped every valve and stop-cock like it was the hand of a friend! Men who felt the gradient through the soles of their boots and heard the pressure in the thrusts of the piston. But nowadays! Nowadays it wouldn't surprise me if the driver of this so-called train wasn't lying back with a glass of brandy in a

London club, watching us on a computer screen and half sloshed out of his upper-class over-educated skull!"

"You're wrong and I can prove it," says the stranger. They stare at him.

At first sight there is nothing unusual in this man whose modest smile seems to apologize for his slightly taller than average height. The large pockets, the discreet epaulets of his well-cut, dove-grey jacket would look equally inconspicuous in a cinema queue or an officers' mess, yet he faces the six pairs of enquiring eyes with a relaxed and flawless confidence which so acts upon two of the women that they sigh with relief.

"Who the hell are you?" asks the old man, and the teacher says, "The driver – I recognize his voice."

"Correct! So you see, I'm not lying back in a London club, I'm here beside you. I really am one of you. May I join you for a moment?"

Taking a small metal frame from a pocket the driver opens it into a stool with a canvas seat, places that in the aisle and sits down facing them. Although his chin now rests on his steeply angled knees he does not look at all ridiculous. Most of the company are impressed.

"I feel so safe," murmurs Mrs Dear, and "Stop scowling Dad, it isn't polite," says the mother, and Mr Dear says, "Excuse me sir, I have said harsh things about British Rail in my time . . . " ("Of course you have" says the driver genially) ". . . but I have never doubted that our trains are the safest in the world and our drivers second to none – if only the trade unions would stop confusing them with promises of Utopian conditions."

"Thank you," says the driver.

"Train driving seems to have changed in recent years," says the teacher in a high clear voice.

"Excuse me madam," says the driver, "I'll gladly explain anything you do not understand after I've had time to . . . to . . . " (and suddenly he looks confused, embarrassed, almost boyish) ". . . you see it isn't every day I have a chance to speak to John Halifax!"

"Eh!" says the old man staring at him.

"You *are* John Halifax, the last of the steam men? Who took three whole minutes off the Bundlon to Glaik run in the great railway race between LMS and the LNER in nineteen thirty-four?"

"You know about that?" whispers the old man with a wondering stare.

"You are a legend in railway circles, Mr Halifax."

"But how did you know I was on the train?"

"Aha!" says the driver waggishly, "I'm not supposed to tell passengers certain things, but to hell with security. The ticket office clerks are not the ignorant gits the public assume. They keep me informed. I used your grandchild's escapade as an excuse to seek you out, and here I am!"

"I see!" whispers the old man, smiling and nodding to himself.

"Please don't get cross, but I need to ask you a terribly personal question," says the driver, "It's about the last great railway race. Do you remember stoking the Spitfire Thunderbolt up the Devil's Kidney gradient with only three minutes to reach Beattock Summit or the race would be lost?"

"Oh I remember!"

"Were you, on that heroic drive, exhausting yourself, torturing yourself, pressing out every ounce of your energy and intelligence merely to advertise the old LMS?"

"No, I was not."

"Then why did you do it? I know it wasn't for money."

"I did it for steam," says the old man after a pause, "I did it for British steam."

"I *knew* you would give me that answer!" cries the delighted driver, and Mr Dear says, "Excuse me, may I butt in? You see Mr Halifax and I kick, you might say, with opposite feet. He's left and I'm right. I didn't realize before now that we are essential parts of the same body. Captain Rogers has made me see that for the first time. Mr Halifax, I am no toady. When I offer you my hand I am merely demonstrating my respect for you as a man. I am apologizing for nothing. But here . . . is . . . my hand. Will you . . .?"

Leaning sideways he stretches out his arm across the aisle.

"Put it there!" says the old steam man and they

shake heartily. Suddenly all three men are chuckling and the mother and Mrs Dear smiling happily and Patsy bumping boisterously up and down. But in a voice used to calling unruly classes to order the teacher says, "Perhaps Captain Rogers will now tell us why he isn't with his engine!"

The passengers stare at the driver who shrugs, spreads his hands and says, "I'm afraid, madam, the heroic age of engine driving went out with steam. The modern engine (we call them traction units nowadays) only requires my attention from time to time. Our speed and position are being monitored, at the present moment, from headquarters in Stoke-on-Trent. It's a perfectly safe system. All Europe uses it. And America."
"But in America last week there was a terrible accident . . ."
"Yes, madam, through a fault in their central data bank at Detroit. These big continental systems are all far too centralized. The British branch of the system has enough autonomy to prevent such accidents here. So you see, although I am not drinking brandy in a London club (I never touch alcohol – doctor's orders!) I look more like a Piccadilly lounge-lizard than like the legendary John Halifax here. My main task is to keep down the buffet prices and stop passengers bickering with one another. And I'm not always successful."
"I think you succeed splendidly!" says Mrs Dear enthusiastically.

"Hear hear!" says her husband.

"You're certainly good with passengers –" says the teacher, and, "You aren't the fool I took you for, I'll give you that," says the old man.

"Thank you John," says the driver gratefully, "With all due respect to the other passengers here, it is your opinion which counts with me."

The chiming is heard then the firm friendly voice says, "Good day good people, there is no cause for alarm. This is your driver Captain Rogers speaking. Here is a special message for Captain Rogers. Will he please proceed to the traction unit? Proceed to the traction unit. Thank you."

"Pre-recorded, of course?" says the old steam man knowingly.

"Quite right," says the driver, who has risen and pocketed his stool, "If the traction unit is empty when a message comes from HQ, the graphic print-out activates that announcement and – duty calls! I'm sorry I have to return to my cabin. I'll probably find a rotten stock-market report that forces me to raise the price of tea again. I hope not. Goodbye John."

"Goodbye, er . . .? "

"Felix. Goodbye good people."

He departs leaving nearly everyone in a relaxed and social mood.

"What a nice man!" says Mrs Dear, and the mother agrees. Mr Dear announces, "He was informed – and informative."

The teacher says, "But the situation he laid bare for us was not reassuring. Nobody is driving this train."

"Utter rubbish!" cries Mr Dear, "There's a . . . there are all kinds of things driving this train, data-banks and computers and silicon chips all ticking and whirring in the headquarters at Stockton- on-Tees."

"Stoke-on-Trent," murmurs his wife.

"Shut up dear, the town doesn't matter."

"Well," says the teacher, "I find it disturbing to be driven by machines which aren't on board with us. Don't you, Mr Halifax?"

The old steam man ponders a while then says hesitantly, "I might have done if I hadn't met the driver. But he's an educated chap. He wouldn't take things so casually if there was any danger, now would he?"

"Madam," says Mr Dear, "We are actually far far safer being driven by a machine in Stoke-Newington. No thug with a gun can force it to stop the train, or divert us into a siding where terrorists threaten our lives in order to blackmail the government."

They sit in silence for a while then the teacher says firmly, "You are both perfectly right. I have been very, very foolish."

And then the chiming sounds and they hear that soothing voice again.

"This is your driver, Captain Rogers. We are

cruising above the Wash at a speed of two hundred and sixty-one kilometres per hour, and the Quantum-Cortexin ventilation system is keeping the air at the exact temperature of the human skin. So far our run has gone very smoothly, and I deeply regret that I must now apologize for a delay in the anticipated time of arrival. An error in our central data-bank has resulted in the 1999 Aquarian from Bundlon to Shaglow running on the same line as the 1999 Aquarian from Shaglow to Bundlon. The collision is scheduled to occur in exactly eight minutes thirteen seconds . . . " (there is a brief outcry which nobody notices they contribute to) ". . . at a point eight and a half kilometres south of Bagchester. But there is absolutely no need for alarm. Our technicians in Stoke-Poges are working overtime to reprogramme the master computer and may actually prevent the collision. Meanwhile we have ample time to put into effect the following safety precautions so please listen carefully. Under the arms of your seats you will find slight metal projections. These are the ends of your safety-belt. Pull them out and lock them round you. That is all you need to do. The fire-prevention system is working perfectly and shortly before impact steel shutters will close off the windows to prevent injury from splintered glass. At the present moment television crews and ambulances are whizzing toward the point of collision from all over England, and in cases of real poverty British Rail have undertaken to pay the ambulance fees. I need not say how much I personally regret the inconvenience, but we're in this together, and I appeal to the spirit of Dunkirk . . ." (the old steam man snarls) " . . .that capacity for calmness under stress which has made us famous throughout the globe. Passengers near the traction unit should not attempt to move to the rear of the train. This sound . . . "(there is a sudden swish and thud) ". . . is the noise of the doors between the carriages sealing themselves to prevent a stampede. But there is no need for alarm. The collision is not scheduled for another, er. . . seven minutes three seconds exactly, and I will have time to visit your compartments with my personal key and ensure that safety precautions are being observed. This is not goodbye, but *au revoir*. And fasten those belts!"

With a click his voice falls silent and is followed by bracing music of a bright and military sort, but not played loud enough to drown normal conversation.
"Oh what can we do, Dad?" asks the mother, but the old steam man says gruffly, "Attend to the child Miriam."
The metal projections under the arm-rests pull out into elasticated metal bands with locking buckles at the ends.
"I don't want to be tied up!" says Patsy sulkily.
"Just pretend we're in an aeroplane, dear," says the mother, locking the belt, "Look Grampa's

doing it! We're all doing it! And now. . ." says the mother in the faint voice of one who fights against hysteria ". . .we're all safe as houses!"

"Dear, I . . .I'm terrified," says Mrs Dear.

Her husband says tenderly, "It's a bad business, dear, but I'm sure we'll pull through somehow."

Then he looks to the teacher and says quietly, "Madam, I owe you an apology. This rail system is more inept, more inane, more . . . altogether bad than I thought possible in a country like ours."

"You can say that again!" groans the old steam man.

"I want to get off this train," says the child sulkily and for while they listen to the quiet rushing of the wheels.

Suddenly the teacher cries, "The child is correct! We should slow the train down and jump off it!"

She fumbles with the lock of her belt saying, "I know our speed is controlled by wireless waves or something but the motor – the thing which makes the wheels turn – is quite near us, in the traction unit, could we not . . ."

"By heck it's worth a try!" shouts the fireman, fumbling at his belt, "Just let me get at that engine! Just let me get out of this . . . This bloody belt won't unlock!"

"Neither will mine," says Mr Dear in a peculiar voice. None of the seat belts unlock. The teacher says forlornly, "I suppose they call this security."

But the old steam man refuses to sit still. Pressing his elbows against the chair-back he hurls his massive bulk forward again and again, muttering through gritted teeth, "I won't – let – the bastards – do it!"

Though the belt does not break it suddenly gives an inch then another inch as a rending sound is heard inside the upholstery.

Then somewhere a door swishes open and the driver is beside them asking smoothly, "What seems to be the problem?"

"Quick Felix!" says the old steam man, relaxing for a moment, "Get me out of this seat and into your cabin. I want a crack at the motor. I'm sure I can damage it with something heavy. I'll shove my body into it if that will let some of us off!"

"Too late for heroics John!" declares the driver, "I cannot possibly allow you to damage company property in that wanton fashion."

His voice is clear and cold. He wears a belt with a gun holster, and has his hand on it. He stands at ease but every line of his body indicates martial discipline. All stare aghast at him. The old man says, "You . . . are . . . insane!" and flings himself forward against the belt again but the driver says, "No, John Halifax! You are insane and I have this to prove it."

He draws his gun and fires. It explodes with a thud, not a bang. The fireman slumps forward though his belt holds him in the chair. Mrs Dear starts screaming for help so he shoots her too. There is now a dim, sharp-smelling smoke in the air but the survivors are too stunned to cough. They stare at the driver in a way which clearly upsets him, for he waves the gun about saying testily, "I have NOT killed them! This is an anaesthetic gas pistol developed for use against civilians in Ulster, does anyone else want a whiff? Saves emotional stress. A spell of oblivion and with luck you wake up in the ward of a comfortable, crowded hospital."

"Thank you, no!" says the teacher icily, "We prefer to face death with open eyes, however futile and unnecessary it is."

The chiming sounds and the familiar voice announces that this is Captain Rogers speaking, that three and a half minutes remain before impact, that Captain Rogers should proceed immediately to the guard's van. With a touch of his earlier, gentler, apologetic manner the driver says goodbye, and explains he is forced to leave them because someone must survive the wreck to report it at the official enquiry. The mother cries, "Oh sir, please unlock Patsy and take him with you, she's only a little child . . . " but Patsy screams, "No Mum, I'm staying with you Mum, he's nasty nasty nasty!" so the driver says quickly, "Goodbye good people," and leaves.

When the door snaps shut behind him the mother says in a kind, careful, trembling voice, "You know The Lord Is My Shepherd, Patsy.

Let's say it, shall we?" and together they murmur,
"The Lord is my shepherd. I shall not want. He
maketh me to lie down in green pastures. He
leadeth me beside the still waters . . ."
With a clang of metal sheeting the windows are
blotted out by shutters.
"Pitch, pitch dark," says Mr Dear, "They haven't
even allowed us light."
He is clasping his wife's body so that her
unconscious head rests upon his shoulder, and he
finds some comfort in this pressure.
"I know it is a small mercy," says the voice of the
teacher, "But I'm glad that military band no longer
sounds."

In the darkness the throbbing of the train
wheels is more audible and the mother and child
pray louder to be heard above it, but not much
louder. They reach the end of the prayer, start
again at the beginning and continue reciting till the
very end.
"Do you remember," says the teacher suddenly,
"When every carriage had a communication cord
that any traveller could pull and stop the train?"
"Yes!" says Mr Dear with a noise between a groan
and a chuckle, "Penalty for improper use £5."
"Once upon a time every small boy wanted to
drive a train when he grew up," sighs the teacher,
"And in rural communities the station-master
played a rubber of whist on Sunday evenings with
the schoolmaster, the banker and the local

clergyman. I remember a bright spring morning on the platform at Beattock. A porter took a wicker basket from the guard's van and released a whole flight of carrier pigeons. I remember signal boxes with pots of geraniums on the sills."

Mr Dear sighs and says, "We had a human railway once. Why did it change?"

"Because we did not stick to steam!" says the teacher firmly, "We used to be fuelled by coal, our own British coal which would have lasted us for centuries. Now we depend on dangerous poisonous stuff produced by foreign companies based in America, Arabia and . . ."

"You're wrong," says Mr Dear, "These companies aren't based anywhere. I've shares in a few. The people running them have offices in Amsterdam and Hong Kong, bank accounts in Switzerland and homes on several continents."

"So that is why we are driven from outside," cries the teacher, getting excited, "None of US is in charge of us now."

"Some of us pretend to be."

They hear the faint distant scream of an approaching train siren. It swells so loud that the teacher is forced to yell over it, "But nobody is really in charge of us now! Nobody is in charge of us . . ."

She has braced herself for an explosion, but does not hear one, or hears and forgets it immediately. The train is no longer moving. The

blackness enfolding her is so warm and snug that
for a moment she dreams she is at home in bed. When she hears the voice of a child calling drowsily, "Mummy . . . Mummy . . . " she almost believes it is her own. The voice of a mother answers on a wondering note, "I think – Patsy – we're going to be all right."

A moment later the teacher, like other passengers on that train, hears the start of a truly huge and final explosion, but not the end of it.

MISTER MEIKLE – AN EPILOGUE

AT THE AGE OF FIVE I was confined to a room made and furnished by people I had never met and who had never heard of me. Here, in a crowd of nearly forty strangers, I remained six hours a day and five days a week for many years, being ordered about by a much bigger, older stranger who found me no more interesting than the rest. Luckily the prison was well stocked with pencils and our warder (a woman) wanted us to use them. One day she asked us what we thought were good thing to write poems about. The four or five with opinions on the matter (I was one of them) called out suggestions which she wrote down on the blackboard :–   *A FAIRY*
A MUSHROOM
SOME GRASS
PINE NEEDLES
A TINY STONE

We thought these things poetic because the verses in our school-books mostly dealt with such small, innocuous items. The teacher now asked everyone in the class to write their own verses about one or more of these items. With ease, speed and hardly any intelligent thought I wrote this :–

A fairy on a mushroom,
sewing with some grass,
and a pine-tree needle,
for the time to pass.

Soon the grass it withered,
The needle broke away,
She sat down on a tiny stone,
And wept for half the day.

The teacher read this aloud to the class, pointing out that I had not only used every item on the list, I had used them in the order of listing. While writing the verses I had been excited by my mastery of the materials. I now felt extraordinarily interesting. Most people become writers by degrees. From me, in an instant, all effort to become anything else dropped like a discarded overcoat. I never abandoned verse but came to spend more time writing prose – small harmless items interested me less than prehistoric monsters, Roman arenas, volcanoes, cruel queens and life on other planets. I aimed to write a novel in which all these would be met and dominated by me, a boy from Glasgow. I wanted to get it written and published when I was twelve, but failed. Each time I wrote some opening sentences I saw they were the work of a child. The only works I managed to finish were short compositions on subjects set by the teacher. She was not the international audience I wanted, but better than nobody.

At the age of twelve I entered Whitehill Senior Secondary School, a plain late 19th-century building of the same height and red sandstone as adjacent tenements, but more menacing. The playgrounds were walled and fenced like prison exercise yards; the windows, though huge, were disproportionately narrow, with sills deliberately designed to be far above our heads when we sat down. Half of what we studied there impressed me as gloomily as the building. Instead of one teacher I had eight a week, often six a day, and half of them treated me as an obstinate idiot. They had to treat me as an idiot. Compound interest, sines, cosines, Latin declensions, tables of elements tasted to my mind like sawdust in my mouth: those who dished it out expected me to swallow while an almost bodily instinct urged me to vomit. I did neither. My body put on an obedient, hypocritical act while my mind dodged out through imaginary doors. In this I was like many other schoolboys, perhaps most others. Nearly all of us kept magazines of popular adventure serials under our school books and when possible stuck our faces into *The Rover*, *Hotspur*, *Wizard* and highly coloured American comics, then new to Britain, in which the proportion of print to pictorial matter was astonishingly small. Only the extent of my addiction to fictional worlds was worse than normal, being magnified into mania by inability to enjoy much else. I was too clumsily fearful to enjoy football and mix with girls, though women and brave actions were what I most wanted. Since poems, plays and novels often deal with these I easily swallowed the fictions urged on us by the teachers of English, though the authors (Chaucer,

Shakespeare, Jane Austin, Walter Scott) were far less easily digested than *The Rover* et cetera.

Mr Meikle was my English teacher and managed the school magazine. I met him when I was thirteen. He became my first editor and publisher, and a year or two later, by putting me in charge of the magazine's literary and artistic pages, enabled me to edit and publish myself. There must have been times when he gave me advice and directions, but these were offered so tactfully that I cannot remember them: I was only aware of freedom and opportunity. Quiet courtesy, sympathy and knowledge are chiefly what I recall of him, and a theatricality so mild that few of us saw it as such, though it probably eased his dealings with those inclined to mistake politeness for weakness. I will try to describe him more exactly.

His lined triangular face above a tall thin body, his black academic gown, thin dark moustache, dark eyebrows and smooth reddish hair gave him a pleasantly saturnine look, especially as the carefully brushed-back hair emphasized two horn-shaped bald patches, one on each side of his brow. While the class worked quietly at a writing exercise he would sit marking homework at his tall narrow desk, and sometimes one of his eyebrows would shoot up into a ferociously steep question mark, then sink to a level line again while the other eyebrow shot up. This suggested he had read something terrible in the page before him, but was now trying to understand the writer's frame of mind. Such small performances always caused a faint stir of amusement among the few who saw them, a stir he gave no sign of noticing. Sometimes, wishing to make my own eyebrows act independently, I held one down with a hand and violently worked the other, but I never managed it. Outside the classroom Mr Meikle smoked a meerschaum pipe. He conducted one of the school choirs which competed in the Glasgow music festivals. His slight theatrical touches had nothing to do with egotism. As he paced up and down the corridors between our desks and talked about literature he was far more interested in the language of Shakespeare, and what Milton learned from it, and what Dryden learned from Milton, and what Pope learned from Dryden, than in himself.

Not everyone liked Mr Meikle's teaching. He did not stimulate debates about what Shakespeare or Pope said, he simply replied to any question we raised about these, explained alternative readings, said why he preferred one of them and went on talking. Nor did he dictate to us glib little phrases which, repeated in an essay, would show an examiner that the student had been driven over the usual hurdles. He let us scribble down what we liked in our English note-books. This style of

teaching seemed to some as dull as I found the
table of elements, but it just suited me. While he
told us, with erudition and humour, the official
story of English literature, I filled note-book after
note-book with doodles recalling the fictions I had
discovered at the local cinemas, on my parents'
bookshelves, in the local library. I was not
ignoring Mr Meikle. While sketching doors and
corridors into the worlds of Walt Disney, Tarzan,
Hans Andersen, Edgar Allan Poe, Lewis Carroll
and H G Wells I was pleased to hear how the
writers of *Hamlet*, *Paradise Lost*, *The Rape of the
Lock* and *Little Dorrit* had invented worlds which
were just as spooky. I was still planning a book
containing all I valued in other works, but one of
these works was beginning to be Glasgow. I had
begun to think my family, neighbours, friends, the
girls I could not get hold of were as interesting as
any people in fiction – almost as interesting as me,
but how could I show it? Joyce's *Portrait of the
Artist as a Young Man* suggested a way, but I
doubted if I could write such a book before I was
seventeen. Meanwhile Mr Meikle's voice often
absorbed my whole attention. I remember
especially his demonstration of the rhetorical
shifts by which Mark Anthony in *Julius Caesar*
changes the mind of the mob.

My private talks with Mr Meikle took place
before the class but out of its earshot. We could
talk quietly because my head, as I stood beside his

desk, was level with his as he sat leaning on it. I remember telling him something about my writing ambitions and adding that, while I found helpful suggestions in his teaching and in the music, history and art classes, the rest of my schooling was a painful hindrance, a humiliating waste of time for both me and my teachers. Mr Meikle answered that Scottish education was not designed to produce specialists before the age of eighteen. Students of science and engineering needed a grounding in English before a Scottish university accepted them, arts students needed a basis of maths, both had to know Latin and he thought this wise. Latin was the language of people who had made European culture by combining the religious books of the Jews with the sciences and arts of the sceptical Greeks. Great writers in every European language had been inspired by Roman literature; Shakespeare only knew a little Latin, but his plays showed he put the little he knew to very good use. Again, mathematics were also a language, an exact way of describing mental and physical events which created our science and industry. No writer who wished to understand the modern world should ignore it. I answered that Latin and maths were not taught like languages through which we could discover and say great things, they were taught as ways to pass examinations – that was how parents and pupils and most of the teachers viewed them; whenever I complained about the boring nature of a Latin or mathematical exercise nobody explained there could be pleasure in it, they said, "You can forget all that when you've been through university and got a steady job." Mr Meikle looked thoughtfully across the bent heads of the class before him, and after a pause said he hoped I would be happy in what I wished to do with my life, but most people, when their educations stopped, earned their bread by work which gave them very little personal satisfaction, but must be done properly simply because their employers required it and our society depended upon it. Schooling had to prepare the majority for their future, as well as the lucky few. He spoke with a resignation and regret I only fully understood eight or nine years later when I earned my own bread, for a while, by school-teaching.

This discussion impressed and disturbed me. Education – schooling – was admired by my parents and praised by the vocal part of Scottish culture as a way to get liberty, independence and a more useful and satisfying life. Since this was my own view also, I had thought the parts of my schooling which felt like slavery were accidents which better organization would abolish. That the parts which felt like slavery were a deliberate preparation for more serfdom – that our schooling was simultaneously freeing some while preparing the rest to be their tools – had not occurred to me. The book I at last wrote described the adventures of someone a bit like me in a world like that, and though not an autobiography (my hero goes mad and commits suicide at the age of twenty-two) it contained portraits of people I had known, Mr Meikle among them. While writing the pages where he appeared I considered several pseudonyms for him. (Strang? Craig? McGurk? Maclehose? Dinwiddie?) but the only name which seemed to suit him was Meikle, so at last I called him that. I was forty-five when the book got published and did not know if he was still alive, but thought he would be amused and perhaps pleased if he read it.

And he was alive, and read it, and was pleased. He came to my book-signing session at Smith's in St Vincent Street, and said so. It was wonderful to see him again, as real as ever despite being a character in my book. Of course his hair was grey now, his scalp much balder, but my head was greying and balding too. I realized he had been a fairly young man when I first saw him in Whitehill, much younger than I was now.

Three years ago I got a note from Mr Meikle saying he could not come to the signing session for my latest novel, as arthritis had confined him to his home. He had ordered a copy from the bookshop, and hoped I would sign it for him, and either leave it to be collected by Mrs Meikle (who was still in good health) or bring it to him myself.

I phoned and told him I could not bring it, as I was going away for a month immediately after the signing session, but I would inscribe a copy for Mrs Meikle to collect, and would phone to arrange a visit as soon as I returned. He said he looked forward to that.

I went away and tried to finish writing a book I had promised to a publisher years before. I failed, came home a month later and did not phone Mr Meikle. He was now one of many I had broken promises to, felt guilty about, wanted to forget. When forgetting was impossible I lay in bed remembering work to be finished, debts to be paid, letters to write, phone-calls and visits I should make. I ought also to get my false teeth mended, tidy my flat and clean the window facing my door on the communal landing. All these matters seemed urgent and I often fell asleep during efforts to list them in order of priority. Action only seemed possible when I jumped up to fend off an immediate disaster, which Mr Meikle was not.

Suddenly I decided to visit him without phoning. It seemed the only way. The sun had set, the street-lights shone, I was sure he was not yet abed, so the season must have been late in the year or very early. The close where he lived was unusually busy. A smart woman holding a clipboard came down and I was pressed to the wall by a bearded man rushing up. He carried on his shoulders what seemed a telescope in a felt sock. I noticed electrical cables on the stairs, and on a landing a stack of the metal tripods used with lighting equipment. None of this surprised me. Film making is as common in Glasgow as in other cities, though I did not think it concerned Mr Meikle. It did. His front door stood open and the cables snaked through it. The lobby was full of recording people and camera people who seemed waiting for something, and I saw from behind a lady who might have been Mrs Meikle carrying round a tray loaded with mugs of coffee. Clearly, a visit at this time would be an interruption. I went back downstairs regretting I had not phoned first, but glad the world was not neglecting Mr Meikle. I even felt slightly jealous of him.

A while after this abortive visit I entered a public house, bought a drink and sat beside a friend who was talking to a stranger. The friend said, "I don't think you two know each other," and introduced the stranger as a sound technician with the British Broadcasting Corporation. The stranger stared hard at me and said, "You may not know me but I know you. You arranged for a whole BBC camera crew to record you talking to your old school-teacher in his home, and did not even turn up."

"I never arranged that!" I cried, appalled, "I never even discussed the matter – never thought of it!"

"Then you arranged it when you were drunk."

I left that pub and rushed away to visit Mr Meikle at once. I was sure the BBC had made a mistake and then blamed me for it, and I was desperate to tell Mr Meikle that he had suffered intrusion and inconvenience through no fault of mine.

Again I entered his close and hurried up to his flat, but there was something wrong with the stairs. They grew unexpectedly steep and narrow. There were no landings or doors off them, but in my urgency I never thought of turning back. At last I emerged onto a narrow railed balcony close beneath a skylight. From here I looked down into a deep hall with several balconies round it at lower levels, a hall which looked like the interior of Whitehill Senior Secondary School, though the Whitehill I remembered had been demolished in 1980. But this was definitely the place where Mr Meikle lived, for looking downward I saw him emerge from a door at the side of the hall and cross the floor toward a main entrance. He did not walk fast, but a careful firmness of step suggested his arthritis had abated a little. He was accompanied by a party of people who, even from this height, I recognized as Scottish writers rather older than me: Norman MacCaig, Iain Crichton Smith, Robert Garioch and Sorley Maclean. As they accompanied Mr Meikle out through the main door I wanted to shout on them to wait for me, but felt too shy. Instead I turned and ran downstairs, found an exit and hurried along the pavement after them, and all the time I was wondering how they had come to know Mr Meikle as well or better than I did. Then I remembered they too had been teachers of English. That explained it – they were Mr Meikle's colleagues. That was why they knew him.

But when I caught up with the group it had grown bigger. I saw many Glasgow writers I knew: Morgan and Lochhead and Leonard and Kelman and Spence et cetera, and from the Western Isles Black Angus and the Montgomery sisters, Derick Thomson, Mackay Brown and others I knew slightly or not at all from the Highlands, Orkneys and Shetlands, from the North Coast and the Eastern Seaboard, Aberdeenshire, Dundee and Fife, from Edinburgh, the Lothians and all the Borders and Galloway up to Ayrshire.

"Are all these folk writers?" I cried aloud. I was afraid that my own work would be swamped by the work of all these other Scottish writers.

"Of course not!" said Archie Hind, who was walking beside me, "Most of them are readers. Readers are just as important as writers and often a lot lonelier. Arthur Meikle taught a lot of readers that they are not alone. So did others in this mob."

"Do you mean that writers are teachers too?" I asked, more worried than ever.

"What a daft idea!" said Archie, laughing,

"Writers and teachers are in completely different kinds of show business. Of course some of them show more than others."

I awoke, and saw it was a dream,
though not entirely.

NOTES, THANKS AND CRITIC FUEL

DEDICATION
This book is inscribed to Tom Maschler because in 1989 he suggested I write another book of stories; to Xandra Hardie because she reminded me of his suggestion; to Morag McAlpine because she gave me the home where I wrote it.

HOUSES AND SMALL LABOUR PARTIES
This tale is informed by three sources: five weeks as a joiner's labourer in the summer of 1953; talks with my father who, after a spell of manual labour, worked ten years as a wages and costing clerk on Scottish building sites; a paper by A J M Sykes called *Navvies: Their Work and Attitudes* published in *Sociology*, Volume 3, Number 1, by The Clarendon Press, Oxford, January 1969.

THE MARRIAGE FEAST
This tale was inspired by the *Memoirs* of Kingsley Amis published by Hutchinson in 1991, and especially by the account of his meeting with Dylan Thomas.

FICTIONAL EXITS
This gives two examples of people overpowered by strong organizations, one of them fantastic, one which happened. The true example is included because its mad logic harmonized with the fantastic. It should not be read as propaganda

against our police for the following reasons.
1. Most of the police I meet are polite and helpful. I also know a detective who enjoys my fiction.
2. Propaganda, like pornography, is a low class of art. The Bible and the writings of Virgil, Dante, Shakespeare, Milton, Shelley, Dickens, Tolstoy et cetera often denounce or promote social organizations, but readers who notice these bits usually find them dull or offensive.
3. Although High Court judges have recently released people unfairly imprisoned by our police the police are less to blame than those who have forced bad working conditions on them. Our police used to have a good reputation because they seldom arrested folk without evidence against them. It was illegal for them to break into our houses without a warrant signed by a justice of the peace; illegal to arrest without charging the arrested person with a crime; illegal to quote as evidence what they said we had said, if we denied it and no independent witness confirmed it. As a child in a Yorkshire primary school I was taught that these safeguards of British liberty were guaranteed by the Magna Carta.

In 1982 the government abolished these safeguards because Irish Republican Army bombers were getting away with murder. In effect the government told the police, "Fight the dirty bastards as dirtily as you like. Arrest people on suspicion and get the evidence afterwards. Up and at them!" So careful search for evidence was put second to quick results, and since our police now had some of the freedom enjoyed by Stalin's police they got quick results. After IRA bombings in Guildford and Birmingham clusters of Irish were arrested, tried, convicted and jailed. The British government, press and people were sombrely glad; the police were relieved. Had they worked carefully, without using torture and perjury to back their suspicions, innocent Irish would have walked free but the guilty might not have been caught and the government would have looked impotent. Conservative governments willingly declare their impotence when confronted by unemployment and widespread wage reductions (their strongest supporters are enriched by these) but when confronted by violence they prefer injustice to looking impotent.

The lack of old police restraints allows many more than the Irish to be falsely accused and punished. It let some muddled policemen break in on a blind man, knock him down and have him fined for it. I use this event to make my story funnier, not for propaganda purposes. If you dislike such mistakes vote into power a radical party which will restore the ancient safeguards.

THE TRENDELENBURG POSITION
Although the writing of this story was helped by my dentist, Mr J Whyte of Glasgow G12, it does

not reflect his political, religious and sporting preferences.

MISTER MEIKLE – AN EPILOGUE
Mr Arthur Meikle was born on April the 17th, 1910, and died on March the 30th, 1993. Sometime before his death he allowed me to use him as a character in my last tall tale, read the result, and approved. He also kindly sat for his portrait in the illustration. Thousands of former pupils know him as a real good teacher of English who worked in Whitehill Senior Secondary from 1939 to 1956, Hutcheson's Boys' Grammar from 1956 to 1975. He also edited *Julius Caesar* in the Kennet Shakespeare series, published by Edward Arnold Ltd in 1964. This very cheap little book has been reprinted more often than all the editions of my books added together. The easily read, richly informative notes have the wise, thoughtful tone of Mr Meikle's teaching voice, making it both an excellent school-book and acting script.

I also thank Archie Hind for letting me describe him as one of Mr Meikle's colleagues, though the two never met.

TYPOGRAPHY
The patient skills of Donald Goodbrand Saunders, Michelle Baxter and Joe Murray set up all of this book except the illustrations.
Goodbye!